Omen Amen

Jenny Ackland

Clink
Street

London | New York

Published by Clink Street Publishing 2021

Copyright © 2021

First edition.

ISBNs:
978-1-913568-02-3 paperback
978-1-913568-03-0 ebook

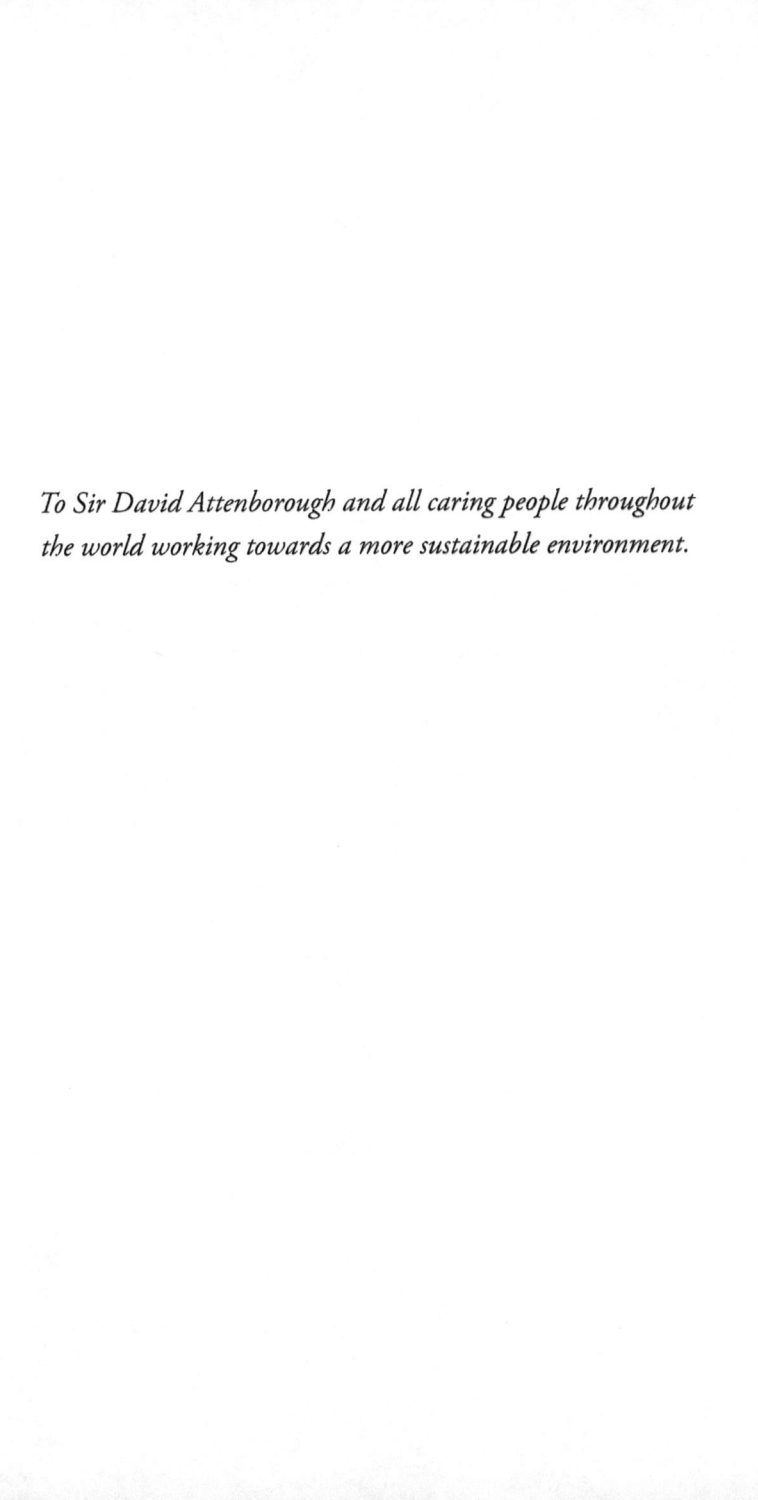

To Sir David Attenborough and all caring people throughout the world working towards a more sustainable environment.

PART ONE

One

This world was shooting, looting,
and polluting;
Inevitably shrinking,
With no one thinking.

The year 4000
The Growth of Area Leaders.

In the time of approximately 4000 time present there are still some human throwback remains. These relics are the progeny of the few humans who survived the annihilation of that devastating time.

The decision to phase them out was passed by the Area Leaders, who were, and remain, the controllers of the area groups throughout the Worldmass orbit. All the throwback corpses were retained for research. Some of the elderly surviving humans had the remnants of faults, most of which have since been eliminated. It is hoped that, within the near future, all genetic mutations will have been destroyed. The Area Leaders have the knowledge that they have survived themselves by being in possession of superior genetic constitutions.

We, the Area Leaders representing different areas of the world landmasses, are investigating the contents of many Time Capsules. We will use the knowledge from these to make decisions about any that might be used for research. The Time Capsules were found deep underneath the earth-soils when intensive digging was being undertaken for further construction of living occupation.

There are many millions of Time Capsules each with an indication of the contents. We, as Area Leaders will ensure that the knowledge of the time past will be used only if it is considered beneficial to our peoples.

The first container to be opened was one tightly filled with evidence of the skeleton of the peoples of millennia past.

One particularly noticeable characteristic of these remnants from time past concerns the skeletal formation of the bones of the spine. The remnants show thoracic bones have evolved to curve outwards so that the neck appears bent. We assume this is the result of the apparent obsession the peoples of the years, approximately 1980 onwards, for observing the content of screens, often for many consecutive hours.

We have been interested to see the development of virtual reality. This was another poorly thought out invention which was rapidly manufactured without the essential consideration of impact. We are confident our knowledge of historical errors will ensure our future will be faultless. Unfortunately, this residue of peoples from the years approximately 2000 to 2050 had indications of further numerous unacceptable attributes. As a result of this research, the future is being completely re-designed and manufactured to avoid the following: obesity, mental health issues, poor physical ability, learning and performing problems, poor eating habits, drug and gaming addictions, emphasis on appearance, tattoos, genetic mutations and addiction to technology. We will investigate all the millions of facts in the Time Capsules with great intensity.

We are increasingly in the knowledge that there were negative living environments for these peoples. There was much violence on all sizes of screens. This could be the reason why the peoples of those times past, by visually witnessing so much aggression, accepted this as normal behaviour.

There are positive signs that most of our citizens are accepting the radical decisions being made on their behalf. As the process of elimination of all unproductive attitudes and characteristics progresses, all choices are gradually being superimposed by the Area Leaders.

As all these undesirable characteristics have been exposed to us over many centuries we have been increasingly confident that success in achieving the perfect and productive citizen will come to fruition in the near future. As we gather further information about the peoples of more than two millennia time past, we are increasingly convinced that our decisions are correct.

One Time Capsule that we opened was identified with the label 'Health and Medicines'. In past time there was much valuable research into disabling conditions. Many of these, it is apparent to us, were caused by negative lifestyles. The peoples were allowed to eat extremely unhealthy processed foods containing many chemical additives, some of which were essential vitamins and minerals but we in time present ensure all the necessary nutrients are added from natural sources. There appears, from the Time Capsules, to be an increasing concern about the level of sugars added to the foods. There was an epidemic of obesity from the second millennium. In our opinion we think poor eating was caused by poor habits and laziness. There should have been no excuses for feeding the populations with foodstuffs that was making them ill.

We are not in the knowledge of the reasons why these forms of living endured but are aware that there must have been complex causes. As we have eliminated poor nutritional standards we will not investigate further into this category, unless we feel we can learn from it.

We were impressed by the intensive research being undertaken to cure and prevent many illnesses. The Time Capsules contained numerous intensive projects aimed at eliminating serious diseases and birth defects. The Area Leaders respect this to a high degree but are disappointed that there was not more overall prevention of disease awareness by the populations. We saw examples of horrifying birth defects of which we have no knowledge and we admired the dedication to keeping these alive although in time present we do not have any such mutations. During the last two millennia much progress has been made in diagnosis and treatment of illnesses. Skin is now robotically touched for an instant diagnosis and remedy, which is delivered by specifically designed mobile robots thus keeping our systems instantly involved in productive on-task operations. This decreases the prospect of redundancy. Of course problems with health are almost eradicated, and the robotic remedial warehouses working efficiently.

In one of the Time Capsules, under the same medical category, there were very unusual visual records showing people undertaking some sort of ritual. This involved the insertion of mounds of soft material being inserted into a female's breasts. We are given the information that this is called breast implant surgery. We can see no logical reason for this procedure.

There were also visual images, usually of female faces, being cut and shrunk in some strange and unnecessary procedure. We learnt that new facial parts could be altered or added to. This was an important piece of information for us in time present. We are adamant that we have no need for this. This was reinforced by the statistical records showing the majority of those undergoing these procedures were inclined to unhappiness and the result gave them no meaningful improvement in mental health. As our populations are living a full working lifetime there are no requirements for replacements, breasts or any other healthy part of the anatomy.

Many of our robotic servers fulfil the tasks performed by the specific spectrum of specialisations. It leaves the populations time for individual skill development which, in turn, can be used for training younger members to replace those no longer useful. Our robotic systems are complex and cover all areas of potential need. If any new areas of reaction are necessary, the robotic fleets can be automatically induced with total and instant input. In this way the Area Leaders continuously monitor the complete requirements of the vast majority of the Worldmass populations. Detailed investigations are undertaken into every possible accessible area of the Landmasses, the Area Leaders keeping to a strict timetable with as few interruptions as is possible.

The research into the Time Capsules is also considered an essential part of statistical knowledge which, in time, will produce many indications of the hazards we will avoid in the future. We have found a record of statements from the past, one of which was, 'It's an accident waiting to happen'. We do not know the origin of this but it seems to give a prediction of an impending disaster. We know a tragedy occurred but there appears to be few significant details. This lack of a definite cause leads us to believe there must have been a steady growth of poorly thought out actions by the Ancient people which accumulated and combined to trigger the eventual annihilation of the majority.

When researching into one of the Time Capsules one of the most toxic areas of damage during the previous centuries had been the increasing number of extinctions of animals, birds and insects. All the preventive techniques we have put into action have had only a minimal effect. We are in the process of advanced research into the genetic regeneration of these creatures. The Area Leaders are becoming increasingly aware that the patterns and sequences of life are interrelated with these ancient beings. All the records recovered from the damage thrust on the populations of many centuries past show a diversity of people and animals that is constantly causing amazement. We will retain and develop any that are necessary to our present needs. Unfortunately there is much poisonous matter impregnated within the remnants of the human remains. We will be cautious when investigating the possible causes and outcomes.

We have, however, researched many areas to establish the causes of many centuries of worldwide pollution. The outcome was that an emergency legal agreement was drawn up between all parties throughout the majority of the world. The purpose of these charters was to prevent any destruction of the systems on which all life depends. The Area Leaders take full responsibility for the progression and implementation of these agreements.

It is becoming increasingly apparent to us that there was a certain inevitability in the lack of progress in a multitude of categories of life during past millennia. There seems to have been little questioning, only confusion and uncertainty by the vast majority of the populations. A passive acceptance of conditions challenging a positive 'lifestyle' as it was named, was fed to the majority of the world's peoples, followed by no meaningful actions to ensure improvement.

The many Time Capsules named as 'The Environment' were enriching to our experiences of the time millennia past. We ourselves, led by the Area Leaders, have numerous of these records kept in secure containers. Inside these are stored the history of millions of categories of animals, insects and plants. An immense amount is known about sustainable development from the devotion of our chosen sections of the population. We, always led by the Area Leaders, have made vast strides into the development and maintenance of new and clean methods of life for our emerging populations. Many other aspects of our research during the last 1000 years have also been safely stored.

As moonstream inhabitants have a similar structure of population control and development as on Earthmass there are essential restrictions on the number of our populations transported to the moonplanet. There may be a superior procedure of existence experienced by those populations on the moonplanet as the length of time of the established populations is relatively new and not under the intense scrutiny necessary on our Earthmass. We are constantly learning about the priceless materials and energy sources contained within the Moonmass. We will take as much time as necessary to ensure no errors are made when utilising and developing these resources. We are the fortunate owners of established facts relating to the Moonmass and are of the opinion that, if the inhabitants of the Worldmass of 4millennia past had the ability to act on information about their future, they might have survived.

They were aware that the moonplanet was between four and six billion years in time past to their present. They also had the knowledge that the planets were interlocked in history. In their 'wisdom' they decided to 'map' the seabed, an indication of how little they grasped the urgency of solving their present problems on their Earthmass.

Our Moonmass supports life adequately as we transport all that is vital for sustainability and we have concentrated our research into the Time Capsules containing historical information about the environment.

We learnt that, in the Worldmass about a two millennia time past, there were many obvious dangers with warnings frequently impressed on the populations. Some areas of the world were guilty of treating this information with contempt, continuing to pollute the atmosphere and oceans. This is inexplicable to us at this time. All this information of the past is giving us more proof that life was not sustainable in the longer term.

We have not manufactured any non-biodegradable products for centuries but it has proved impossible to remove it completely from the land and oceans.

Another difficulty we are experiencing at this present time is that of the condition of the earthsoils. More than two millennia time past, once again, repeated warnings were expressed concerning the quality of the earthsoil being damaged, to such an extent that any plants essential to human life were severely depleted. Increasing amounts of fertilizers and herbicides were added which, as time passed, decreased the effectiveness. Many basic robotic machines were implemented and the quantity of produced food maximised.

However, this was increasingly difficult and we have maintained and increased the research into, and production of, artificial food.

At that time too, insects were declining at an increasing rate and creatures familiar for many centuries are now extinct. An example of this is the honey bee. Without this essential insect, pollination does not happen and an increased level of research is being undertaken to substitute the function of many insects including the honey bee. We have been forced to substitute many of the original insect life with genetically resourced imitations. This has not been as successful as we require as mutations have started to appear for no logical reason. Robots are being employed to destroy these and delete the cause.

The Area Leaders have a nil tolerance of any fault within our research outcomes and the sections of the population responsible for not succeeding are returned to positions of inferiority.

There are records, of approximately 2050 years past, when horrendous acts of violence were perpetrated between peoples.

Some millions were annihilated with no controls being possible. The reason wasn't obvious to us. It was, and still is, a worrying time and innovative controls are being developed and maximised throughout the Worldmass to ensure this is not repeated.

The use of fossil fuels was made illegal in 2100 but only achieved due to the obvious fact that, if the world was to survive, all energy needed to come from renewable sources. A massive investment of time and the item called Money was granted to various parts of the world where there was an abundance of solar power, water and wind energy. The records show the immense amount of improvement these developments stimulated. Unfortunately, this was too late and the world fell into disruption, discord and disillusionment.

We learn, from a capsule named as 'Energy' in time past from the year 2019, there was a proposed geothermal energy project in an unusual development named a 'The Eden Project'. This project was in an area named as Cornwall which was the most southerly part of the landmass named as the United Kingdom. There were images of large bio-domes which replicated the differing climates, soils, ecosystems, animal habitats, plants, trees and food production of each individual landmass.

The geothermal project consisted of drilling deep into the earth and piping cold water into the depths. The outcome was that the cold water would be heated by the high temperature and be returned to the surface. There were only superficial details of this project but we were impressed by the unexpected innovation. The aim was to provide energy for many of the population. At least some of the peoples must have been in possession of information relating to the imminent danger of the approaching energy shortages.

The future was appalling and from then on the world was an insecure and threatened place. The Area Leaders have confidence that the decisions being taken in present time are correct and will result in a cleanly functioning population that will fulfil all the requirements of the present Worldmass and Moonmass.

Every three years new Area Leaders are chosen and the present inhabitants of these positions are directed into research. We have found that this mechanism achieves the best results for the future innovations and standards of perfection that we will meet.

Two

Seasons of mist and mellow fruitfulness
Close bosom-friend of the maturing sun,
Conspiring with him how to load and bless
With fruit the vines that round the thatch-eves run;
To bend with apples the mossed cottage trees
And fill all fruit with ripeness to the core;
To swell the gourd, and plump the hazel shells
With a sweet kernel to set budding more,
And still more, later flowers for the bees,
Until they think warm days will never cease,
For Summer has o'er -brimmed their clammy cells.

'To Autumn'
– John Keats

As time progressed through the years from 2000 to the present, struggling through the succeeding centuries, the records show societies throughout the world becoming increasingly discontented, functioning competitively and aggressively. The peoples were unhappy and the levels of self-destruction were rapidly increasing. There was much frustration and passivity as food became scarce and people were increasingly substituted by robots in every area of life skills. Peoples could be seen walking vaguely and purposelessly about with a machine attached to their ears. Young people were increasingly joined up to machines and their obsession caused much distress.

There appeared to be no methods by which this could be intercepted and peoples' abilities to make contact with each other shrank to a minimal level.

As the centuries passed it became clear that the rapid development of technology had a negative and damaging effect on the population which was irreversible. This encouraged us to invest our energies into robotic substitutions and avoiding the need for mundane interaction between peoples. The Area Leaders have all the controls necessary to ensure our peoples do not find themselves in any inexplicable situations. We, The Area Leaders, are satisfied that progress is being made to design a better and more productive world.

The Area Leaders devoted a limited length of time to one of the Time Capsules names as 'Entertainment'.

One particularly damaging occupation from the past was the manipulation of the people into meaningless activities. There were many screens from which pictures of people involved in very confusing scenes were transmitted to the millions engaging in watching this activity.

One of the most prominent 'Entertainments' appears to have been the promotion of something called 'Betting'. This involved exchanging the item named as 'Money' and receiving a ticket on which there were a sequence of numbers.

If the individual who had exchanged 'Money' for the ticket chose the previously decided numbers correctly, that person would win a great deal of this 'Money'. This made them ecstatic. This was named 'The National Lottery'. Some of the proceeds of this activity was given to charities. Even this appears illogical to us. We aim to provide everything our people need in every respect.

Under the category of 'Betting' there were some inexplicable facts we had difficulty in understanding. There were many of the peoples betting 'Money' on the winner of different competitions, horse racing, car racing, football, and numerous screen games.

We have little interest or experience of these activities but have gained knowledge of some negative outcomes.

Much 'Money' was lost and, frequently, obsession followed. Many of the people involved in this 'Betting' activity had their lifestyles destroyed, having no 'Money' left to exchange for essential items. Another activity we found under the 'Entertainment' category was the involvement in something called 'Game Shows'. These are productions we find difficult to comprehend as they represent yet another transitory undertaking whereby people enter into various tedious tasks in order to win this item named 'Money'.

We curtailed our research into this particular Time Capsule as we found nothing that would be of any significant use to us.

It is increasingly apparent that there was, at that time, an immense emphasis on judging the individual by what is now considered superficial values. We have eliminated all of these visual stimuli as the damage they caused was widespread and lasting. The Time Capsules we have found have provided us with invaluable sources of information that we are studying in depth. Much of the content is inexplicable to us, but we can learn from mistakes of the past and utilise any information that might be valuable. This, up to time present, has presented us with very little material of a positive nature.

One of the Capsules, named as 'Europe', contained information relating to the years 2016 onwards. The populations were asked if they wished to separate from the adjacent land areas. We find this illogical and followed the procedure with amazement. This total area, identified as Europe, had many other adjacent landmasses as members.

The 'United Kingdom' wished to curtail its membership. There had been over seventy years of peace in this area so it must have been a provocative demand from the United Kingdom. We are grateful to have learnt the dangers of non-cooperation and we work continually towards changing the conditions of any area that experiences discontent.

In time past, there were divisions within world areas we find difficult to understand. We know that wars were continuous and world peace never achieved. Our study has shown that there were divisions between the areas named as North and South Korea, India and Pakistan, North and South Ireland, East and West Germany, Israel and Palestine and walls built within one area to prevent peoples travelling from one place to another. There are others we are still investigating so we can continue to learn from these past mistakes and guarantee not to repeat them. We have the knowledge that these attitudes caused wars and a lack of tolerance.

We also have found the records of exploded salt mines. These were used to store the nuclear waste of many centuries ago and we are still investigating the cause of the explosions. There is still an immense amount for us to learn and instruct our future peoples. We have confidence that, with dedication, we can achieve further tremendous improvements.

At time present we are in the knowledge that there are certain areas in possession of banned weaponry hidden within our landmasses. Although we know these exist, we are unable at this time to locate them with precision. We know there are mass killing weapons being stored with the intention of protecting a particular area. We have received the information from the appropriate Area Leaders overseeing this. We know it is essential that we totally isolate these remote areas and destroy any unacceptable substances. We are constantly aware, from the Time Capsule records, that possession of mass destruction weaponry does not promote peaceful coexistence. However, the speed that our advanced robotic control defence systems are developing is proving a positive advancement and the Area Leaders are confident of imminent success.

It is incumbent on the Area Leaders to conserve and protect all the information about these weapons possessing the ability to destroy the Worldmasses many times over. All peoples are instructed to obey the orders of the Area Leaders and to maintain a peaceful relationship with all other areas. The Area Leaders are hoping that the powerful robotic defence mechanisms, in the final stages of development, will eliminate any chance of increased aggression. If all Worldmass areas possess robotic shields it will ensure the peaceful continuation of our programmes, the outcome of which will be a perfect world driven by automatic procedures which, in turn, will result in a happy and peaceful population.

We opened a Time Capsule with the title 'Religion'. As we have no knowledge of this category we were interested to become initiated. Researching into the past shows that promoting differences between peoples caused much anger, mistrust and violence. The conclusion we drew, after intensive consideration, was to give the populations no overall choice whatever. With this knowledge, we have decided that there will be no idols to encourage worship. Many centuries past there were beliefs indicated by a name and which encouraged an idolising pattern of behaviour from a very young age. It was named 'religious belief' and involved early indoctrination. It was proved to be the cause of many millions of deaths as the different religions fought each other. We have eradicated this. There is no need for any inclusion of these 'Religions' in present time.

Further extraordinary facts were found in the Time Capsule of the year 2019. One, in particular, was the speech given by a young girl of sixteen years. She was most articulate and warned the world that it was on a damaging course of action. We, the Area Leaders, listened intently as she spoke with passion and integrity about the damage the peoples were inflicting on the ecosystems and the increasing levels of self- inflicted pollution. We know that her predictions must have had some accuracy concerning the eventual destruction we know happened many centuries later. There were many young peoples named as 'Extinction Rebellion' fighters who desperately tried to make their voices heard. We would have been proud to include them in our developing Worldmass.

It is reassuring to us, the Area Leaders, that there were at least a minority of the 'Ancient' peoples trying their best to influence others of the urgency in saving the planet. They showed courage and insight. It is a tragedy that any effective action was too slow. There were many associated problems and it seems to us that the world, in the condition it was at that time, just lost all impetus.

Three

Waves trough-rebound-and fury boil again
Like plunging monsters rising underneath
Who the top like a shaggy main
A moment catching at a surer breath
Then plunging headlong down and down-and on
Each following boil the shadow of the last
And other monsters rise when those are gone
Crest their fringed waves-plunge onward and are past
The chill air comes around me ocean blea
From bank to bank the waterstrife is spread
Strange birds like snow spots o'er the huzzing sea
Hang where the wild duck hurried past and fled
On roars the flood-all restless to be free
Like trouble wandering to eternity.

from *'The Flood'*
– John Clare

The Area Leaders opened a Time Capsule named as 'Global Warming' and the contents were an indication that our decisions were correct.

The four words, repeated many times, were 'Climate Change', and 'Global Warming'. They were a further confirmation that all the predictions by the scientists of the late twentieth century were accurate.

We have seen images of ice melting causing the sea levels to rise and weather patterns to alter. There were scenes of many areas under water and land destroyed. Additional scenes showed ice of 10,000 years of age melting. Surely the people should have acted immediately, as indicated by so many of the experts. To have knowledge and not utilise it indicates extreme ignorance. It was at about this time that the air temperatures rose to levels never experienced before. Every area of the landmasses from the time of these Ancients were affected until the inevitable decline occurred.

We also have evidence that the item called the 'Jet Stream', which dictated the direction the weather followed, radically altered its course. Many weather forecasters warned of the outcomes of this change but, once again, no immediate action followed.

Looking at all the evidence from that time indicates the predictability of disasters. We have repeated scenes of great floods, again caused by the rise in sea levels due to the melting of the ice caps in the north and south apexes. As a result of this we are precisely aware what developments, based on historical research, our decisions must follow.

There was a time when meadow, grove, and stream,
The earth, and every common sight,
    To me did seem
Apparelled in celestial light,
The glory and the freshness of a dream.
It is not now as it has been of yore;-
    Turn whereso'er I may,
By night or day,
The things which I have seen I now can see no more.

'ODE' – *Intimations of Immortality*
– William Wordsworth

The next Time Capsule to be opened was within the section labelled as 'Festivals'. We have no experience of this category of events but were sufficiently stimulated to investigate further.

At an event called 'Glastonbury', which was an annual event attracting many thousands of the peoples, there were many platforms on which people performed on instruments and the crowds got very excited. On one of the platforms the man of great respect, Sir David Attenborough, spoke to the people about the damage being forced on the environment. The devastation of the living environment was caused by the peoples using polluting energy sources, discarding articles that cannot biodegrade and not showing concern for the future condition of the planet. There was much shouting and appreciation of his attendance and the words he used. However, we cannot comprehend the reason following this reaction for there being virtually no response from the decision makers to try to alleviate all the proven environmental damage.

We watched the tapes named as 'Our Planet' which were so interesting to us as it showed all the magnificence of the historical natural world but also warned of the dangerous situations developing. It was another symptom of the devastation developing over the following centuries. We are increasingly determined to avoid repeating any of these profound mistakes. We know, however, much of the richness of the environment has been permanently lost.

There were some records of something called deforestation and this was undertaken to provide the land for growing 'trees' named as 'palm'. This was demonstrated by images of thousands of areas of massive, imposing, green plants being cut down, and substituted by the 'palm tree' that could be grown quickly and utilized as content for many common items used by the Ancients. The product was called 'palm oil'. Deforestation was one of the causes of the decline of the conditions needed to provide healthy living environments. The Area Leaders are learning many essential historical facts that are relevant to their decisions of the present.

The term 'tree' is unfamiliar to us and difficult for us to comprehend but the Time Capsule's contents were of great interest. We have noted the importance that many of the people, named as 'Environmentalists', attach to the word. They give the information to their peoples that the carbon being emitted into the atmosphere can be partially eliminated by these 'trees'. We learn that this carbon is produced by all the travelling machines, aeroplanes, fossil fuel use and other inefficient methods of producing energy. We have made a definite future time allocation during which we will further investigate these items.

The next Time Capsule to be investigated had the label 'Pregnancy and Birth'. We were interested in the historical methods of replacing population numbers. The methodology used appeared very time consuming and uncomfortable for the carrier of the foetus.

We have facilitated an organised method. This is overseen

by the Area Leaders in a strict system. When it is decided to permit a new birth, the clinic has a simple procedure, using superior proven sperm stored throughout centuries. It has been genetically selected by quality and specific projected requirements of the populations. The ovaries producing the ova have been screened in a similar fashion so there is no risk of any contamination. The sperm and ova are then cultured in the laboratory and the donors can collect the matured embryo after nine months. The donors are at liberty to care for the child for six months in the germ-free areas that has everything needed to ensure the child develops in the pre-determined pattern.

We are certain this method achieves excellent outcomes. We have no abnormalities recorded and all the participants must be content.

Looking at records of the years 2000 onwards, the Ancients bear only a small resemblance to our progeny. As words are now becoming redundant, we note that smaller orifices for words to be emitted have evolved. The peoples from the Ancient times have all their receptors in abundance but it was obvious that these have now shrunk as their use, over time, was virtually eliminated. The hands of the Ancients were large and always moving; the hearing organs also much larger than our refinements. The visual organs were also shrinking but our progeny illustrate smaller eyeballs but with increased visual acuity. Our hands have three digits and one very flexible thumb. Our feet and hands are very flat and wide as befits the type of daily movement necessary.

We insist on mandatory daily activities and, apart from the essential water therapy involvement, many non-weight bearing skills are to be enjoyed. All populations will conform to the rigorous exercise routines prescribed. Records will be kept to ensure encouragement is given via their personal internal computer network system. Many opportunities are provided so, by this means, individual satisfaction is guaranteed. We have perfect conditions for all physical exercise, with energy output being recorded in accordance with the necessary input of sustenance. In our exercise systems we have many water-based centres. To be weightless is vital for good health. From birth all of our peoples spend at least a tenth of their daylight in the water-based activity of their choice. The resulting health and energy benefits are monitored automatically and we are satisfied that the results are consistent with our expectations.

We have opened the Time Capsule with the label 'Sport'. This category seems to have been based on competing against one or more other people. We have no need for competition. The ancient records show much discordant behaviour surrounding group events, especially when a ball, stick or racquet was involved. The records list an endless category of these. One in particular, called football, made us confident that our own attitude to physicality was preferable. There appear to be many angry faces, waving of arms and general dissatisfaction.

One of the strange visual experiences we accessed in the Time Capsule was entitled 'The Olympics, 2016'. This was of great interest to us although we were not familiar with the various flags representing the competing areas. We watch this event but decided it was not something we needed to store. There was much jumping, throwing and running. Times and distances appeared to be of immense importance. The 'winners' climbed onto a platform with a disc hung round their necks. These were gold, silver and bronze. There were many thousands of peoples watching and making very loud noises. There were events of colour and noise at the commencement and end of this 'Olympics'. When this event finished, everything was very quiet and movement ceased. Even the enormous buildings, presumably housing the competitors, were empty and silence filled the area.

The only event to which we responded positively was the swimming as all our populations enter into this activity. However we have not been persuaded to have this item called 'competition' as our swimmers must be relaxed and content having no obligation to prove they are better than anyone else. We, as Area Leaders, have a responsibility to make decisions on behalf of our populations that are in their best developmental interests.

Four

The woods are desolate of song-the sky
Is all forsaken in its joyous crowd;
Martin and swallow there no longer fly
-Huge-seeming rocks and deserts now enshroud
The sky for aye with shadow shaping cloud.
None thereof all those busy tribes remain;
No song is heard save one that wails aloud
From the all lone and melancholy crane
Who like a traveller lost the right road seeks in vain.

from *'St Martin's Eve'*
– John Clare

The Time Capsule records indicate in the years 2000 forward there was an abundance of ill-health caused by poor nutritional choices. Some of this was triggered by the production of the food available being very counter productive to good health. Much of it appeared bright orange in colour. It was easy and cheap to access. Our records show many very large peoples walking slowly. This was a time when there was also much poverty even in the most developed areas of the world. In the U.K. there were areas providing an item called 'food banks' for the peoples unable to access any. Once again, the item named 'Money' was the means by which the people could exchange it for food and other essential items. The results of not possessing adequate 'Money' resulted in immense levels of deprivation in living structures and general health.

The U.K. area was advertised as one of the richest in the world so, as learning from other world areas that functioned in a similar fashion, we ourselves have learned not to descend into those extremes of inequality.

Possessing this 'Money' gave the individual high levels of power over other people, living areas, occupations, learning facilities and nutrition. Not possessing 'Money' resulted in some appalling individual cases of existence. Even self-death resulted. Apparently young men were the most likely to end their own life-forms. We are still investigating the causes of this.

After an interval in our research, due to an urgency to ensure all security systems were perfect, we re-established the commitment to the Time Capsules. We identified many visual records of the architecture of those years, between 2000 and the present. These were of an incredible and immense stature and intricate design. There were buildings called palaces and mansions inhabited by people that possessed much of the 'Money' commodity.

In the same capsule we were negatively impressed by opposing scenes. There were many peoples lying on the ground, within sight of the large buildings and cathedrals. We learn that they were homeless. It interested us that the cathedrals were places of so-called 'religion' which was apparently invented to encourage a caring attitude to all others. That is something we are proud to have eliminated as the caring attitude is obviously not something to be developed if it is closely connected to this thing called 'religion'. We were disturbed by the content.

Another Time Capsule with the label 'Celebrity' attracted us by the unknown title. We were perplexed and intrigued by the word.

It took us some time to comprehend the actual meaning of the term. It was prevalent prior to the years 2000 onwards and promoted yet another superficial outlook from many of the populations. Vulnerable individuals were chosen to enter into various self- promoting activities, many of which were humiliating. It appears these competitive 'games' were very popular which does not surprise us as the general behaviour of many of the people appeared very self-concerned. We still have not fully understood the definition of the word 'celebrity'.

Undertaking further study indicates that many of the contestants were indeed classified as 'vulnerable', a word that seems to be attached to many of the bizarre 'Game' or 'Reality' shows. We are still not totally confident as to the precise meaning of this word. The Time Capsule named as 'Entertainment' contains many activities of which we have very little or no experience.

One appalling result from these 'Reality' shows was another outcome which we find difficult to comprehend. Three of the young young people competing killed themselves. Once again we have no ability to establish a reason for this lack of care towards the peoples.

There were several examples of further pointless and damaging activities. We watched several 'games' on screens with meaningless titles to us. The peoples watched these for many of the hours in the day and night. Once again we were affected by the number of instances of violence in the content. Every 'game' we experienced contained scenes of war, cruelty and extreme behaviours. Those participating were fully involved entering into the seemingly endless violent exercises.

We have curtailed our investigation, deciding they were damaging and resulted in negative standards of development.

We have found some more confusing items in the Time Capsule, named as 'History', with various dates following. We eventually decided to open this but there was a certain reluctance based on our previous experience. The contents appear to be of a genuine, ancient historical nature. They relate to approximately the century of the 1700s. All that was left in the capsule was a written page accompanied by visual backups. We were given the information that there were 3000 of the population watching what, we assume, was classified as 'entertainment'. There was a wooden structure from which several people were hanging by their necks. We learnt that these people were being destroyed for committing a 'crime'.

It was difficult to make any judgement but was unpleasant to see so many people watching, mouths open wide. We deduced they were shouting appreciation.

We have learnt that, centuries past, there were many violent acts between peoples. We looked at another image of the bodies of those that had been hung taken to what we have learnt was called the Houses of Parliament, having been 'hung, drawn and quartered'. The Houses of Parliament were the imposing buildings in which many decisions were made by representatives of the peoples. Many laws were instigated in this building.

We learnt that 'hung, drawn and quartered' meant the dead body was cut into four and draped over the railings of the Houses of Parliament. We have made our own decisions about this.

We are thankful that our populations have been indoctrinated to accept the correct standards of living a healthy and productive life.

As has been emphasised, our confidence in the total control the Area Leaders have over the peoples is paramount to our successful development of all our global landmass areas, and we can almost discount the knowledge of remnants of remote dissenters or nonconformists. The overriding factor is that we do indeed have the knowledge of these almost invisible beings and have methods by which we should be able to contain them.

The Area Leaders consistently spend an allocated time in learning about these damaging times in the distant past of the Ancients. It was an indescribably painful time for many of those inhabitants and no surprise when they self- destructed. We are thankful that the Time Capsules show us the numerous appalling systems by which the poor inhabitants existed. We have gained much knowledge and wisdom from them.

Once again we have allocated some time for research into the distant past. We opened a Time Capsule named as 'The Victorians' which described the century named as the Victorian Era which was approximately in the late eighteenth century forwards which, again, showed much inequality between the peoples. There were pictures of many thousands of adults and children being transported to this land by boat to act as slaves, working for the more privileged for virtually no 'Money'. There was a man, eventually, who passed a law in the previously mentioned Houses of Parliament, that stopped this. We cannot understand the level of cruelty from one man against another and are calmly confident that we are providing a better environment. When we have isolated the small sections in remote areas and re-taught them the rules by which we will all live in harmony, total calm and serenity will result. The Area Leaders will work tirelessly to ensure this.

We know it is important to continue to research the Time Capsules and study as much information as possible from the past in order to guarantee an avoidance of any similar mistakes.

Another instance causing incredulity was the knowledge that there were so many examples of the immense difference between those with 'Money' (the rich) and those without 'Money' (the poor). These categories have been eliminated, but in the era of the Victorians, many centuries past, invading and possessing territories, often owned by indigenous peoples, was considered acceptable. Vast sailing ships with sails but no other means of energy, travelled vast distances to lands far from their own to areas of which they had no knowledge. The populations were often badly treated and made to act as slaves. The invaders then decided that these new territories belonged to them and this was repeated many times. These occupied lands, over time, were called 'colonies'. We are certain we have learnt to develop the maximum potential from our peoples without the need to steal capacity from other areas.

The most popular Time Capsules are those named as 'History'. We deduce the reason for the popularity of this specific title is so the Area Leaders can judge the success of all their decisions. Even without the knowledge from the Time Capsules we are confident that the alterations we have made to the expectations of our peoples are justified.

It was learnt that, approximately two and a half millennia time past, many peoples were permitted to travel from across the channel between what was known as France and England, to live in peace with the peoples in the cities of what was called Great Britain. They were called Huguenots and were a creative and inventive breed. The numbers were in excess of 30,000. We would like to think there are genetic remnants of these peoples in time present, as all the information we have been given indicate it was a time of great innovation.

All our peoples are permitted to travel anywhere in our developing lands. Our secure lines of robotic control defence systems ensure every movement is monitored with precision. The result is a pleasing level of passivity.

In another Time Capsule we found evidence of skeletons of extinct creatures called dinosaurs. These were in existence many millions of years prior to time present. What magnificent creatures they were and in existence during the time before humans. We wonder why they became extinct but can find no absolute proof of the reason. It has made us particularly aware of the length of time the planets have existed and our lack of accurate knowledge we possess about the creation of life. We know how it is destroyed, because history has given us numerous examples, but we are accelerating our determination to avoid the pitfalls from the past, and learn more about the creation of the universe in its totality.

Five

So little cause for carolings
  Of such ecstatic sound
Was written on terrestrial things
  Afar or nigh around
That I could think there trembled through
  His happy goodnight air
Some blessed Hope, whereof he knew
  And I was unaware.

'*The Darkling Thrush*' 31st December 1900
– Thomas Hardy

Another visit was made to the Time Capsules; on this occasion one named as 'Diversity and Charles Darwin' was opened. The name of this capsule intrigued us and we were eager to investigate the contents.

We were not disappointed. We learnt that in the years between 1831 and 1836 research was entered into the theory of evolution.

The man named Darwin was dedicated to find reasons for changes in inherited materials. We, the Area Leaders, became very immersed in this theory as we ourselves have made decisions concerning selection of preferred and dominant genetic tendencies.

There was a title for his theories, named as 'Survival of the Fittest'. It was extremely controversial at the time as it threatened religious beliefs. Because his findings were unpopular he did not make them known until 1859. His theory of 'natural selection' was eventually widely accepted as other scientists and biologists supported his findings. The Area Leaders read all this information with great interest. They read about Darwin's many years of experimentation with plants and his travels to an area named as Galapagos, where he found proof that animals also changed over many centuries to adapt to the environment. They became stronger and survived. His results proved that unions between plants and cross fertilisations resulted in a strong survival ability. Many years passed before his theories were widely accepted.

The Area Leaders unanimously decided to use this research in their own developmental processes. It was the first time that they had been fully engaged in the contents of a Time Capsule. They would enable any definitive knowledge to be passed to the relevant systems.

In these systems, knowledge is provided in individually designed computer instructions. These are animated tools, provided and made available to be used from a very young age. We have advanced the simulated learning tasks for each individual appropriate to need and intent, judged by the Area Leaders.

All abilities are assessed and encouraged as the individual matures. Consideration is then given to the optimum output that can be expected from the potential adult and appropriate workloads activated.

Yet another series of facts has emerged from the Time Capsules. This time the subject matter related to air pollution. Most of the peoples were breathing contaminated air and some of the vulnerable were having their potential life-span reduced by a considerable length.

Once again this is difficult for us to comprehend. The pollution was caused by the peoples using toxic materials. As this was known by the Members of the Parliament, representing the different areas, it seems an ignorant and short-sighted situation. This confirms the fact our Area Leaders have a superior awareness of the needs of our populations.

One of the main pollutants was the method by which the peoples travelled from place to place. They used a container called a car but the energy needed to make it move was a poison. Eventually, a cleaner energy was used, called electricity. We, of course, utilise our energy from solar sources, and our storage systems are reaching a standard of perfection of which we are satisfied.

In time past, the records indicate a travelling machine using electricity was invented. This was in time past of 1897. This makes us question why this method was not developed and pursued. Our design of streamlined transportation to the place of work has been one of the most supreme achievements of recent centuries.

The skyline tubular routes result in fast and efficient destintimes. All those being transported know they will arrive punctually. All energy is supplied by solar storage and automatically delivered when needed. By comparison, the Ancients used additional carriers in the skies called aeroplanes and these were exceptionally large, energy inefficient, noisy, polluting and unnecessary.

There was also another scheme which resulted in the destruction of many rich environments, containing thousands of irreplaceable flora and fauna including valuable trees, which seem to be increasingly important. This piece of unnecessary over development was named HS2 and referred to the invention of a high speed capsule travelling from the South to the North of the land carrying people slightly quicker to their destination. An immense amount of added pollution was produced by building this structure, lasting many years. All this we have learnt recently from the Time Capsule contents and from this we know the permanent damage caused. We will not abuse the natural landmasses. There are, however, only poor remnants with which we can work and we are increasingly aware of the need to respect our environment, damaged though it is. We have gained so much from learning to avoid making catastrophic decisions from millennia past. One fact that has shocked us is the loss of over 100 ancient woodlands in order to access land for the high-speed rail link. Yet again this is another sign of the lack of care for the environment.

As we continue to research the Time Capsules, some of which we instantly destroy, there are a few that we retain for historical purposes. The Area Leaders are aware that, since time began, futures depend on present innovation and development. We maintain a consistent attitude to this, therefore retaining any possible material that might be of use to us in time present.

One pioneering project instigated, approximately in the years of 2015 onwards, was one to tap into the geothermal energy from many kilometres beneath the surface. The purpose of this was to harness renewable energy. The Area Leaders were surprised at this rare effort to produce this essential source of supply. The peoples of that era were almost static in the attention that was paid to this vital necessity. Their efforts resulted in provision of electricity from the core of the earth. The length of time taken by this achievement was extensive. The area, known as 'The Eden Project', had already been using this method. This was of interest to us but, with our superior investment in research, know our acquisition of vital energy sources has been successful for many centuries.

We are continuously amazed by the ignorance shown by all the Ancients. They only needed to look up into space to see the source of vital energy supply shining down upon them. With the research undertaken by our dedicated workers, we have been supplied with energy for all our needs for many centuries.

The Area Leaders frequently ask themselves if the decisions made by the Ancients had any residual benefit to the time present. The vast majority of the knowledge gained from the Time Capsules was unfortunately of no use. All the research and time given to these Ancients' decisions resulted in the Area Leaders reacting with almost total disbelief.

As the Time Capsule containing material of an energy and travel category was planned, we allocated some additional time to decide if any of the contents were worthy of further investigation.

Once again, we were disappointed by the contents. It was clear that much emphasis was placed on utilising the space surrounding the Worldmass, rather than improving the actual landmass itself.

There was much attention paid to the design of something named as a 'spaceport'. This was constructed with the intention of allowing rich people a short trip. The aerospace industry was, of course, competitive. There were other peoples spending vast amounts of this 'Money' commodity to ensure they were the first to offer the peoples the opportunity to engage in this experience.

Once again the Area leaders were disappointed at the lack of intensive research of the Ancients. If they, as we have learnt, worked together the results might have been more productive for all the peoples. Travelling for a short time into space for no apparent reason apart from personal satisfaction, was not permitted in our development. We have many researchers and robotic investigators improving and monitoring our systems of travel between planets. We always achieve the highest standards for our peoples as a result.

As we experience further examples of poorly thought out decisions by these Ancients, we gain further knowledge of our own future. There are continuous extremely positive outcomes from the time we spend on selective contents of the Time Capsules.

Our peoples have a genetically engineered ability to adapt to differing environments automatically. As there are no situations in which they feel they have to compete or show superiority they can rely on peacefulness and the populations functioning at maximum capacity. The acceptance of this information by the very minor clusters of remote peoples will complete our statistics.

The Area Leaders have robotic surveillance systems, consistently delivering information in immediate time and, if any extreme or unacceptable event occurs, they have almost perfected the ability to exterminate it.

In a Time Capsule labelled 'Crime' there was visual evidence of peoples having committed an antisocial action. These peoples were locked up in cells, and behaving very negatively. It was apparent that they were under the influence of some poisonous drug. We have not been able to access further information but all that we have seen has made us very uneasy. We find it difficult to understand the reasons for this containment of so many thousands of the peoples. Our decision to prevent any situation in which a person is denied liberty has been one of our most successful developments.

We have learnt that the behaviour resulting in incarceration was called 'crime'. We have eradicated this over many centuries. The vast majority of our peoples have earned our trust and live healthy and productive lifespans. As has been stated, there is an extremely small and remote group of clans indicating the need for intervention. However, the situation is under almost perfect control.

We are perpetually shocked by the lack of involvement exercised by the leaders of times so long in the past. The images show many unhappy situations and it is difficult to understand why the leaders would want to keep an historical record.

There is one image in particular, which impressed our leaders as it was another record of the life experience of so many of the Ancient peoples. There were many of them showing all stages of their development with enormous body mass, so huge that their ability to manoeuvre themselves from one area to another was virtually impossible without a supreme effort. It is apparent that much time was spent watching screens and eating food which appeared to be in a package. We cannot understand why this was permitted. The Ancients did not appear to have much control over their lifestyles.

We find ourselves repeatedly asking ourselves how that situation had developed and if it could have been prevented although we had seen evidence of some of the peoples with an acceptable pattern of behaviours.

There seem to have been little attention paid to changing these, or investigating the reasons causing them.

We have opened a Time Capsule named as 'Knife Crime'. This was recorded for the years between 2000-2025. The criminal statistics of that time saw a vast increase in the numbers of 'knife' crimes. This was another indication that the development of the peoples needed attention. It was in the larger inhabited areas named as cities that these attacks were undertaken. Why the peoples would want to stick knives into each other is a mystery to us.

We asked ourselves if the many hours the Ancients

watched violent acts on screens could be one of the causes. As we do not allow any scenes of violence to occur, in reality or in any other genre, it is a logical conclusion that the Ancients could become brutalised to scenes of aggression and therefore accept it as normal. This is a subject that needs more attention. As the Area leaders find it unpleasant, we will concentrate on finding more useful material. We have been reminded, by the content we have just watched, of the minimal possibility of minor reactions from the remote areas in our landmasses. An increase in concentrated robotic surveillance has been stimulated by this recent experience of the content of the Time Capsule.

We were interested in a Time Capsule named a 'Soaps'. We were hoping for a positive content. Researching this word indicated that this item was used for cleansing. This was an error, as the title, 'Soaps' named a series of screen items representing the lives of the peoples. We decided to look at this, to remedy any error on our part as to the definition of the word 'Soap'. We opened one named as 'Eastenders'.

We watched an image of a person with a weapon, named as a gun. We have the knowledge that this item was used to kill. It is no longer in existence in our populations. There followed much fighting and screaming. We terminated this and opened another 'Soap'. This one was named as 'Coronation Street'. There were images of buildings burning down, peoples getting hit in the face, more shouting, screaming and violence. We terminated this.

The Area Leaders are considering the content of these 'Soaps'. After more careful thought we have again come to the conclusion that the constant exposure to violent images must have a negative effect on peoples of a 'vulnerable' condition. The many examples we have witnessed on the Time Capsule contents, concerning people in negative situations, have led us to the conclusion that violence on the ever-present screens had stimulated a similar reaction from the 'vulnerable'. We are certain that our decision is the correct one.

We are so near to attaining perfection in all areas of our population development that any unacceptable actions must be monitored with precision. Watching the contents of the 'Soaps' has reinforced our decision to demand acceptable behaviour at all times from our populations.

Many of the Time Capsules refer to the two centuries prior to the self-destruction that occurred. We are increasingly interested in the causes, but increasingly suspicious of the reasons for the lack of preventative actions.

We spent some time monitoring the security system performance, in particular the remote areas which have been under some suspicion. Although we are confident when receiving the robotic results, the recent Time Capsule contents have caused a minor anxiety.

Six

I dreaded walking where there was no path
And pressed with cautious tread the meadow swath
And always turned to look with wary eye
And always feared the owner coming by;
Yet everything about where I had gone
appeared so beautiful I ventured on
And when I gained the road where all are free
I fancied every stranger frowned at me
And every kinder look appeared to say
You've been on trespass on your walk today
I've often thought the day appeared so fine,
How beautiful if such a place were mine;
But having nought I never feel alone
And cannot use another's as my own.

'The Passing Traveller'
– John Clare

The Area leaders, drawing on experience, decided to open another Time Capsule. This one was named 'Social Media'. The content was, once again, damaging to many of the 'subscribers'. Numerous insulting messages and threats were passed between peoples. We could only experience the depth of unpleasantness for a limited time and therefore curtailed the session. There were extremely personal images of the very young shared with what appeared to be world-wide consumption. We shut this down. Our pity for the Ancients was growing as so many of the images were of certain subjects that we find unacceptably crude and pointless.

There were many titles of the various categories accessed by the young peoples. Although we should have been prepared for the shocking content, we found ourselves without the ability to react.

There were promotions showing a young person how to end their own life, and other graphic indications of similar horrific instructions which the Area Leaders immediately destroyed.

The Area Leaders had a growing impatience with the Time Capsules due to the abundance of worthless material contained within them. Searching for an allocated time it was decided to avoid any which had an ambiguous label.

One was therefore selected named as 'Red Nose Day.' This was a straightforward name and should have been interesting for research. It was assumed the content would explain all the varieties of nasal protuberances. The Area Leaders were not acquainted with the images which followed. They watched mesmerised by the various colourful dances, musical performances and the level of laughter. They devoted more time to this than intended and were made aware that these performances were all undertaken to raise 'Money' for those needing it throughout the Worldmass. Once again, they were bemused by the contrasting attitudes towards the care of the populations.

As this activity had taken up a considerable time we concentrated the following extended timeslot into the completion of the security connections in the remaining known remote parts of the farthest landmasses. We are obliged that this must take priority.

After we were certain that we had reached the optimum level of security possible for that particular landmass we opened another Time Capsule, named as 'Strictly'. We did not have any experience of this isolated word.

After the recent violent images we had witnessed, we were pleasantly surprised by the content. There were two people together moving to music. This was named as dancing. As we permit our peoples to choose this as one of their physical activities, we recognised it. It was spoiled for us by four people being negative. They were sitting behind a bench and holding up cards on which numbers between one and ten were printed. Each 'judge' held up a numbered card after each pair had finished. We anticipated that, once again, this was a competition. Observation of years long past, from the records deposited in the Time Capsules, we are left with an increasing sense of the profound failures of those peoples. We, the Area Leaders, use our ability to learn from many evidences of misleading decisions made by the Ancients, whose incompetent representatives, 'The Members of Parliament' seemed unable or unwilling to make urgent decisions.

There is actual evidence in the Time Capsules of the 'Houses of Parliament' in the landmass named as 'The United Kingdom'. These buildings were massive stone-built edifices, in which there was much shouting. A huge number of transcripts indicate the words used by these people. Very little appears to have been achieved by these leaders to help the many inequalities and sufferings of many of the population throughout the landmasses. Different landmasses had their own leaders, mainly chosen by the populations. There appear to have been many differing ruling organisations of these landmasses, with more freedom of choice in some areas.

We have simplified the organisation of our landmasses with inflexible levels of expected functioning of our peoples.

There are a multitude of examples of past millennia of differing leadership systems but the Area Leaders have the years between the year2000 and 2050 as The Age of Cruelty. They are still hoping to find evidence of a more productive society and have many years to examine all the thousands of preserved items.

As Area Leaders we are responsible for the peacefulness of our peoples. Many times we have seen examples of the Ancients' existence that we find unacceptable. We find ourselves asking, again and again, 'Why?' The numerous occasions that fighting, violence and unhappiness was experienced by the 'Ancients' peoples is confusing to us. We have learnt over the centuries that it was essential to identify the causes for these conditions. To us, with our advanced knowledge, the cure appears obvious. If the cause was eliminated, symptoms of the malady would could have been destroyed. Observing the many examples of disaffected functioning of the peoples, often with very immature development, has resulted in a very useful research subject. We are aware that improvement in knowledge takes an extended length of time and consider investigating the Time Capsule contents a valuable indicator of future developments.

The decision was taken to open another Time Capsule named as 'Wars.' This was not taken lightly. We were in the knowledge that there was intricate technology in widespread existence in the second millennium. Choices were made to destroy vast numbers of populations and landmasses. There was a competitive concentration on competing in an arms race, which included those of nuclear weaponry. It appears to us that different landmasses were intent on dominating others with the result that the destruction of the world became more probable.

The Area Leaders knew that this was the inevitable outcome and questioned why all the knowledge and experience wasn't used for the eradication of disease, poverty and inequality. The contents of the Time Capsule confirmed the Area Leader's positive opinions of their own systems. They will continue to monitor the Ancients' errors and ensure none are repeated in time present.

We have recently found evidence of the buildings in which these Ancient peoples lived. They were made of bricks with slanting roofs.

Some of these roofs had thermal solar storage panels fixed to them which was one of the first positive signs we have seen that there might have been an environmental interest by these populations. We are, once again, mystified by the lack of urgency this innovative procedure stimulated. We suspect the delay was caused by the ever- present manipulation of 'Money', or the lack of it.

The Ancients eventually comprehended there was a decreasing length of time left for them to rescue the planet. What has become abundantly clear to us is that there were numerous warnings given, spoken by eminent leaders of the environment, that were not taken seriously. Many of the peoples of the Worldmass were concentrating more on survival, as their living conditions appeared to deteriorate.

The Area Leaders made the decision to open another Time Capsule. This stimulated great interest as it was named as 'Academy Report into Forest Fires'. This was a confusing label but stimulated our interest.

The content was a description of the devastating raging forest fires in the Amazon, America, Australia and Portugal named areas.

Seven

There I have sat by many a tree,
And leaned o'er many a rural stile
And conned my thoughts as joy to me,
Nought heeding who might frown or smile
'Twas nature's beauty that inspired
My heart with raptures not its own
And she's a fame that never tires;
How could I find myself alone?

from *'The Flitting'*
– John Clare

In the year 2019, there were vast areas of the Amazonian Rainforest destroyed by fire. As this area was essential to the survival of many people living within it, many countries helped to provide the means to extinguish the flames. However, it appears that many of the fires were started deliberately as the trees were used for 'logging' which was clearing the trees from the earth so it could be used for crops that could be sold.

The indigenous peoples were removed from the land so powerful men could make a great deal of 'Money' from harvesting and selling the products. Another unknown fact was indicated to us. The Amazonian area was vital in the second millennium's efforts to mitigate the effects of the vast amounts of pollution being pumped into the atmosphere. The 'trees' were efficient at absorbing the carbon which was the greatest polluter. We don't produce carbon so have none of the Ancients' problems with this pollutant.

We were impressed by a report, completed by relatively young persons. We increasingly came to the decision that the Ancient young were more enlightened than the older ones. They were certainly more engaged in the subject of their own and their descendants' futures.

We have found more evidence of the buildings in which these peoples lived. They consisted of slabs of bricks and slanting roofs. There were glass openings named as windows, through which light was received. The heating of these living areas was by a gas which, to us, seems inexplicable. There were also energy systems functioning by oil, retrieved from under the earth surface and frequently moved many thousands of kilometres in exchange for 'Money'. Again, this is inexplicable to us as the Ancients only needed to look up into the sky to see where their energy needs were waiting to be utilised. There are also some unacceptable details of an unusual practise named as 'fracking'. This entailed disturbing the layers of rock under the ground in certain areas to allow a certain gas to escape. This had a negative result on the surrounding environment as earth tremors were caused. It appears factual to us that, if the Earthmass is disturbed, the outcomes will be unacceptable. The history of earthquakes has given an abundance of evidence in this respect.

The only reason for this 'Fracking' experiment was for the provision of energy. According to the evidence, this activity had to be curtailed. There was, we have learnt, much Ancient dissent about it. Perhaps there were some older Ancients that possessed a capacity for caring for the environment, although they appear to be in the minority.

We found pictures of the interior of some buildings. The walls had frames in which there were images of patterns and, sometimes, of the Ancient peoples. There were many images of animals which appeared to be domestic and kept in the buildings. We have no records apart from those from the Time Capsules. We can see how important these animals were to the Ancients. Many appear to have been fed better than those sections of the poor peoples. We find this difficult to understand as this must indicate that the peoples must adopt different rules for the varying sections of their populations. The framed images indicated a slight level of positivity hidden in the faces as they appeared passive but not unhappy. We prefer our populations to have total serenity and are working very hard to ensure this progress increases in intensity. We have found some of the contents of the Time Capsules illuminating and an indication of the inevitability of self-destructive actions. We have an approximate date of the gradual decline of vast numbers of the populations. From the data we have acquired we learn of the gradual destruction of the systems needed to maintain life started in the years preceding the twenty-first century. There were numerous symptoms ignored; the most prominent, repeated many times,being the increased temperature of the Earthmass areas and radical changes to the climate. The evidence found indicated these were frequently mentioned and accepted by the majority of the Worldmasses.

We decided to study, in more detail,the information of the Time Capsules with the title 'Climate Change 2020'.

This was the year that the anxiety was increasing because of the frequency of cyclones, hurricanes and rising sea levels. We began to acquire a more specific knowledge of the dangerous conditions the world at that time was trying to fight.

There were commitments by seventy countries to achieve zero carbon emissions by the year 2050. This was clearly not enough. The use of fossil fuels were used at the greatest level by the richest countries. The poorest countries suffered most from the results of the pollution caused by the richest.

We are increasingly aware of how important 'trees' were, with the capacity to absorb pollution, and cannot comprehend how slow the reaction was to the obviously spiralling dangers facing the global populations of 2000 onwards. The knowledge of this was worldwide but not enough urgent attention given to the signs. The effort undertaken by the David Attenborough man to give his long and studious expertise to global areas, of intensive warnings of threats to future survival of the planet, were of profound interest to our research into past mistakes and our total avoidance of them in our future. This was a man the Area Leaders would have respected. We would have promoted him to one of our Area Leaders.

We are fortunate to have research indicating that there are numerous indications of life in the depths of the sea. We have instigated our superior technological expertise to maximise the results to benefit all our populations.

Opening the contents of the many Time Capsules categorised as 'The Environment 'we have watched outstanding images. There were many examples of the colourful and vibrant environments in existence before the decline. We are allocating a considerable amount of time in the near future to study and research all the magnificent contents of these visual records.

The results of investigating the contents of the Time Capsules is using much time and we are only able to absorb a small quantity at each session. The Area Leaders have many other responsibilities to ensure all their duties are undertaken with complete success.

Eight

To see a world in a grain of sand
And Heaven in a wild flower,
Hold infinity in the palm of your hand,
And eternity in an hour.

from *'Auguries of Innocence'*
– William Blake

There are numerous examples of living things of which we have no knowledge and this is an area we will correct. There is a possibility we will learn to utilise some of the remnants of these creatures, plants and other once-living animals.

One memorable scene, transmitted to us from one of the Time Capsules, has remained with the Area Leaders and reiterated our determination not to enter into any of the destructive actions of the past. The scene was of vast areas of land of drought and famine. The people were bowed, emaciated and covered in rags.

This was in a time when many areas had valuable resources. We cannot understand how this was allowed to happen. The people of the richest zones must have been very much concerned with themselves and not interested in the welfare of others. Repeatedly, we ask ourselves why there was no action to change this.

The vast majority of our peoples do not lack in nutrition or safe protective quarters in which to live. All the information we have studied has given us great incentive to proceed along the paths on which we are travelling with increasing confidence.

The Area Leaders allocated a minimum time to absorb the content of the many Time Capsules specified as categorised as 'Sport'.

There were images of two people, within a caged area, fighting each other. At first we were confused by this activity again but were becoming familiar with the scenes of aggression, watched by many other people. This represents, to us, yet another example of the obsession with violence that occupied the populations of time long past. Many of them watched with excitement with mouths opening and closing. Men hurled each other onto the floor and it was apparent that there were no rules.

Yet another meaningless activity we watched in an increasingly detached attitude was of people containers. We already had been informed these were identified as racing cars, travelling as fast as possible around a 'track'. Again this activity was attended by many thousands, again showing much agitation. We thought this represented another pointless action and could not comprehend any positive achievement or value. Travelling as fast as possible to finish at the point at which the car started is incomprehensible to us.

One experience of the numerous 'sporting' activities we watched was the category of 'cricket'. The person talking about the action was using many words of which we had no knowledge. This 'cricket' must have played an important part in the Ancients' existence but we found it rather monotonous.

There was a large green area on which this game was played. Two men in white, with much padding on their legs and helmets on their heads, carried bats and walked to the area of play. This consisted of a strip of flat ground. At each end were three vertical sticks on top of which balanced three smaller ones, horizontally. The Area Leaders were reluctantly fascinated and wondered what was the intention of all the preparation.

There were several men spaced out around the area, but all facing the two by the vertical sticks. Then another man starts to run in line with one of the men by the vertical sticks. He throws a little ball very fast at the man with the bat who lifts his bat, hits the ball and runs to the other end of the strip of land. The man by the other little sticks at the other end runs also so they pass each other and there-fore change ends. This happens many times until there is a loud shout and the ball has knocked the little sticks off the tops of the big sticks and the man batting is 'out' and leaves the area. Another time one of the men standing in the area catches the ball after it has been hit. Again, this means that this hitter is 'out' and has to leave the area. This decision is given by a man in a white coat who seems to be the one in charge. We noticed another man with great pads on his legs and padded gloves on his hands. He also had a helmet on. He was crouching behind the vertical sticks, catching the ball if the hitter missed it. This all seemed rather time-con-suming to us but, reluctantly, we found ourselves rather mesmerised. This 'cricket' continued for many hours and possibly days but we could not spare the time to observe it more than we considered necessary.

There was evidence of a method of control of the number of times the batter ran from one end to the other. This consisted of a board on which there were many systematic indicators of the number of times this happened. There were changes to the men throwing the ball also, sometimes it was thrown in a looping action and at other times it was very fast. We were pleased to see that there were no instances of violence. There were populations watching. Their responses were well controlled.

There were also people commenting on this procedure and we, as Area Leaders, felt obliged to listen intently as there might have been information that could be judged as useful for research.

Unfortunately, in unison, the response of The Area Leaders was laughter. This is a reaction we do not encourage unless in extreme circumstances and we were all taken by surprise at our concerted reaction. The cause was the labels given to the positions around the area that the men in white were spread. These labels were, unusually for us, incomprehensible. There was a man standing at 'silly mid-on', one at 'short leg' and another at 'long leg'. There were others but we found ourselves 'laughing', almost uncontrollably, and therefore suspended the activity. There were no further indications of valuable knowledge that we could pass on to our peoples and therefore our involvement ceased.

The Area Leaders were silent as they returned to their duties. We do not understand why there should be such an extreme degree of reaction to some activities and a calm response to some others.

The Area Leaders thought this activity named as 'cricket' was one of the better examples but there was a chance of tedium being experienced. The actual physical effort was minimal from the majority of those involved and the calorific intake would have to be adjusted if we decided to allow our populations to participate in something similar.

The Area Leaders decided unanimously to leave the Time Capsule for some time as the urgency of security statistics was programmed. The robotic artificial intelligence reactors were indicating an immediate need for updating.

As this was achieved to the Area Leaders satisfaction, they found the next section allocated to the Time Capsule. Once again this was under the title 'Sport', with a sub-title 'Golf'. There was an image of an immense open green space. There were hills and pits of sand, flags on poles varying distances apart and two women carrying bags of sticks. The women each took one stick out of their bags and hit a tiny ball out of sight. This was followed by the other woman repeating the action. The Area Leaders found themselves uttering little sniggers. There appeared to be no reason for this occupation.

As with the 'cricket' activity, there were people commenting on the action. Once again we were overcome by the words used. For some reason the extinct names of birds were used. 'Eagle', 'birdie' and 'albatross' were heard. When a 'hole in 'one', was heard we were even more perplexed but decided to terminate the images when 'bogey' and 'double bogey', 'making the 'cut' and 'chipping' were heard. All these words made no logical sense to us.

These people were spending their time on such strange activities. All the faces looked dull and lacking in animation. However, it was decided to continue investigating this 'golf'. As with cricket we found a certain amount of interest developing into these bizarre habits of the Ancients. The women repeated this activity and again each took a little white ball and hit it with a long-handled stick into the horizon. Once again they strode off, presumably looking for them. This was repeated until a flat green space was reached, on which a flag fluttered on a pole. Then a different stick was chosen out of the bag.

Again the women took it in turns to hit the ball, although much more gently. Repeatedly, the aim appeared to be to get the little white ball to enter the little hole in the green area in which the pole was fixed. When this was achieved the women picked their balls out of the hole and moved on to another area to repeat the activity. We were tempted to shut this imagery down but were impressed at the time these people spent patiently on such a strange activity.

There were eighteen holes into which these women eventually succeeded in dropping their balls. The Area Leaders noticed that this game was very serious and the faces of the woman were without expression, which was strange as this was an activity taking many hours to complete. This lack of movement in any meaningful capacity puzzled the observers but interest was soon terminated and once again, the Area Leaders found themselves overcome with a desire to laugh. This was quickly suppressed and normal conduct was once again achieved.

The Area Leaders decided to destroy this evidence as it appeared repetitive, although they had become slightly transfixed by it. It seemed to have a calming and tranquillising effect on them. They decided it would not benefit the populations.

There was another reason for discarding this experience. The time spent watching the golf meant other duties had been downgraded. The Area Leaders knew there were no residual spare landmass capacities to use even if a decision to include this weird sport in the general activities was to be permitted. All viable landmasses were at a premium.

The Area Leaders had a common feeling that they were neglectful in their duties but avoided communicating this between them as anything harmful.

There were some scenes, witnessed within the Time Capsules that caused the interest level to increase. One was a scene of mountains with people climbing to the summit. We ourselves, as Leaders, have made investigations into the highest terrains but to utilise the possible potential in the space, energy and research categories. At time present the development of technological expertise was rapid and won the majority of attention from the peoples, simultaneously trying to avoid the world's resources being abused.

From the time past of 2050 research into Artificial Intelligence resulted in many forms of employment being undertaken by robots. We have learnt from the information gained from the Time Capsules that human resources must be sensitively considered. We are confident that the vast majority of our populations have satisfactory work experiences and the environment provided is calm and productive. Our use of robotic systems is carefully controlled and consideration given to the effect on the populations in the essential employment categories. The Area Leaders are fully informed of all situations that might be needing attention.

In the Time Capsule of the year 1970, there was a record of what was termed the first 'test tube' baby. It gives us pride to know that we do not have to experiment in this area, having perfected procreation. There are no abnormalities in our resulting foetuses. This achievement has taken many centuries to perfect. Increasingly, as we watch and absorb the knowledge from time past, we have confidence in our decisions.

Nine

The golden harvests spring; the unfailing sun
Sheds light and life; the fruits, the flowers, the trees,
Arise in due succession, all things speak
Peace, harmony, and love. The universe,
In natures silent eloquence, declares
That all fulfil the works of love and joy,-
All but the outcast man.

'Nature and Man'
– Percy Bysshe Shelley

One of the most recent examples found in the many Time Capsules entitled 'The Environment', was further information concerning a large image of an insect called a bee. This is extinct as are all the other types of the bee category. Once again there was evidence that these insects were made extinct by the lack of concern the populations gave to the habitat of the bee and other vital insects. The overuse of the capacity of the soil had a negative impact on the wildlife as the poisons sprayed on the land was killing it. Of course we know the result was the inability of the peoples to use the land productively and their failed efforts at regeneration.

Soil erosion and degradation were the inevitable outcomes of neglect and mistreatment of one of the vital resources necessary to support life.

Once again one of the most interesting contents of the Time Capsules was a programme concentrating on the items named as 'trees'. The group of Area Leaders watched the images of these gigantic items with wonder. They had watched the information contained in the Time Capsule named as 'Amazon' but were pleased to receive further details. There were many descriptions of these magnificent plants.

One fact was learnt and was a surprise to us as, by the year 2050, the landmasses of the United Kingdom were committed to a carbon neutral environment and this was partially dependant on the planting of 1.5 billion trees. We had watched the information from the 'Amazon' Capsule and suspected that no action would be taken, but at least some of the world landmasses were making a positive move.

Additional cheap energy processes were proposed, but wind and wave energy supply was very expensive and development was inconsistent. We suspect the damaging past caught up with these plans before the effect could be of value.

In the year 2019 the climate was considered to be in a state of emergency. In our opinion the years between 2019 and 2050, should have seen immense development towards minimising the damage already forced on the environment. It is obvious this didn't happen.

We found the Time Capsule containing images of how the land supported green plants, bushes, hedges and grasslands very absorbing. We were affected greatly. This resulted in silence as we saw, one example after another, the most wonderful statuesque trees, covered in green, brown and red fragile shapes named as leaves. All these trees were of many different varieties shapes, sizes colours and textures.

We were intent on the content and the beauty of them but increasingly confused by the Ancients' inability to nurture them. We learnt that these trees had many purposes, including being used for the making of tables and chairs. The product from the wide girths could also be burnt to enable the Ancients to have heat. We watched as men with loud cutting machines drilled through the trunks of these trees. This was followed by a crashing and splitting sound as one smashed onto the ground. This was repeated many times.

The Area Leaders stopped watching. They knew the content of that particular Time Capsule was something vital in the destruction of the environment. There were no specific details of the century that this tree devastation occurred.

Area Leaders took their leave as quickly as possible, again in total silence. There was no communication between them as they returned to their duties. Some time passed before another visit was planned.

The decision was unanimously taken to research more of the topic named as 'Sport', mainly to find out if there were any that would be worth pursuing. They had little confidence in the Ancients' ability to engage in an activity of lasting value, but hoped to experience the rare feeling of 'laughter' again.

One activity was named 'Cycling'. This involved a frame, with a seat on it, balanced on two wheels. There were pedals to turn the chain which in turn rotated the wheels. This was the best example of a sport that the Ancients had devised. The peoples could use this invention to transport themselves without using any other forms of polluting energy. It was decided not to destroy this evidence. However, there were scenes of these cyclists sharing a wide flat surface with enormous carriers of different purposes. We received information that the cyclists were going to 'work' and were often at risk as the large carriers appeared to be threatening the space that the cyclists were using.

Then the scene moved to what appeared to be a competition. Cyclists were in an arena with a sloping surface, trying to cycle faster than the others. There were many of the peoples watching and making noises. The Area Leaders appreciated that a high level of physical skill was involved to avoid the competitors falling off. Once again they felt a fascination creeping over them and rationed the activity to a short allocation of time. They did not think there were reasons to include this competitive 'cycling' in any of their mandatory activities for their peoples in time present.

The Area Leaders decided to permit themselves one more 'Sport' and 'Grouse Shooting' was opened. This appeared to be static at the introduction and we watched with anticipation. We had no knowledge of 'grouse' but learnt that they were small birds. Then we saw a series of very small cages in which these birds were housed. Spirits fell as we gradually saw some these flying birds released into the openness. To our horror, later, some people with large sticks beat the growing, green plants and the birds flew out to be shot by some other people. Many times we have questioned the occupations of the Ancients in the category of 'Sport' and cannot make sense of the activity. To breed little birds for the purpose of killing them must be considered another bad reflection on these peoples' attitudes.

There was a statistic of 50,000,000 of non-native red-legged partridges, grouse and pheasants being bred specifically and kept in unnatural habitats for this purpose.

Again we, the Area Leaders, were silent. We decided that there must be at least one positive example that we could experience without finding ourselves judging negatively.

The Area Leaders found a Time Capsule named 'Zoos'. This word was meaningless but the decision was made to persevere with the research. This was the correct decision and we saw a multitude of creatures that have been extinct for many centuries. These animals were of vastly different sizes, colours and shapes. We concentrated on the category of 'Mammals'. We learnt that mammals fed their own young and that some ate other animals and some only ate vegetation, which appeared to be growing plants.

We were told that Zoos were in existence because many of the animals were becoming extinct and that it was the intention to try to breed from those in captivity. When they were at the correct time in their development they would be freed into their normal habitat. This was of complete interest to us and we began to have a small amount of respect for these Ancients. It was clear that there were some that possessed a caring attitude to the environment and the many millions of, now extinct, species.

We saw many people exchanging the money commodity for the experience of walking around these zoos. There were many small people with a contented expression on their faces. These, we understood, were the small members of the peoples and each seemed to belong to a small unit. We saw an immense variety of animals, of great beauty and grace. They were very well cared for and the peoples having the occupation of feeding and looking after these amazing creatures also had contented faces. At the completion of our allocated time all the Area Leaders were, once again, silent. They found a mixture of respect and confusion uppermost in their minds. It was now abundantly clear that these Ancients had caring peoples within their populations.

Ten

The poetry of earth in never dead:
When all the birds are faint with the hot sun,
And hide in cooling trees, a voice will run
From hedge to hedge about the new mown mead—
That is the Grasshopper's. He takes the lead
In summer luxury; he has never done,
With his delights, for when tired out with fun.
He rests at ease beneath some pleasant weed.
The poetry of earth is ceasing never:
On a lone winter evening, when the frost
Has wrought a silence, from the stove there shrills
The Cricket's song,in warmth increasing ever,
And seems to one in drowsiness half lost,
The grasshopper's among some grassy hills.

'On The Grasshopper and Cricket'
– John Keats

The decision was made to open the Time Capsule containing information named as 'Entomology'.

Very quickly we were absorbed by the content and had confirmation that the poisoning of the earth was one of the causes of the Ancients extinction but were increasingly informed that there must have been numerous others. The millions of insects species were an essential part of the chain of life for the Ancients. We learnt that, once destroyed, birds had their food source removed. We were told of the vital interdependence between the animals, insects and plants and ultimately all populations. Once again we learnt about the importance of all varieties of bees and insects and the role they played in fertilising plants. We found this information immensely gratifying for the simple reason that it confirmed our knowledge. To have proof indicates that we have made the correct decisions in ensuring our populations do not repeat the same horrendous errors. There were numerous items of information, including the fact that many fossils, including those of insects, had been found 400million years in past time. Fossils were the preservations of insects, animals, and even humans from a time so long past that even we, the Area Leaders, have difficulty in processing. We realise that many of the living beings, for millions of years, must have depended on each other for food. The insects ate green plants. Other insects and animals ate the plant-eating insects and then other animals use these as food. There was a definite pattern to this behaviour and we were in admiration of some of these Ancients for this information which had interested us profoundly.

The Area Leaders decided to concentrate on the protection and alarm system updates throughout the Worldmasses before continuing the research into the Time Capsule contents. As this was closely monitored by automatic robotic cell systems, this was rapidly accomplished. The Area Leaders returned to the Time Capsules, choosing carefully. They did not want to repeat the negative effect the damaging tree situation had posed.

They chose a memory from the years 2000 onwards,

hoping for a positive experience. The example they saw was of popular activities concerning the existence of large rooms full of exercise machines. The Area Leaders saw the individuals doing many unusual movements, losing much body water and, again, having intense and serious expressions. They came to the conclusion that the Ancients were unfulfilled for most of their time as living organisms.

'My subject is War, and the pity of War
The poetry is in the pity'.

Part of draft of a collection of war poems, written by Wilfred Owen, which he hoped to have published in 1919. He was killed at the very end of the war.

During centuries in the distant past, we now know about the numerous wars. Many of the population were killed or seriously injured. We do not allow any contentious violent behaviour. We have seen individuals with artificial limbs and other major injuries. There are records of these disabled peoples in chairs with wheels, appearing to compete against each other.

There are many other instances where these damaged people engaged in activities together. There is much evidence from a Time Capsule with the title 'Invictus Games'. Many peoples with limbs missing and other serious disabilities can be seen having competitions in different sports. We eventually receive the information that all these injuries were caused by fighting in 'Wars'.

A high level of enjoyment was apparent from all the contestants.

It is incomprehensible to us that, in times past, millions of peoples killed and maimed each other. We, in the time present, have virtually perfected the co-operation of zones, resulting in an almost total peacefulness.

The Area Leaders opened a Capsule with the title 'Race'. We had a certain amount of trepidation as we have a premonition that this will refer to the colour of an individual's skin colour. We were correct in our assumption.

It was apparent that, in the nineteenth century, there was much hatred between peoples of different race and skin colour. We have no records of time prior to this.

In time past, individuals were judged by the colour of their skin.

In one African zone, peoples with dark skin were not allowed to sit in a travelling machine with white skinned peoples. All activities were segregated and peoples with non-white skin treated with many humiliations.

A black man, with the name Mandela, was imprisoned for many years as he tried to win freedom for his black peoples. Eventually he was freed and became the leader of an African zone. He fought for equality and respect for all non-white peoples. In the twenty-first century he was loved and respected by many world leaders. After he died there was still much work to be done and black people were still treated poorly in many zones.

It is not surprising that all the hatred and resentment between the peoples at that time gradually added to the growing ferment resulting in the devastation of which we now have knowledge.

There are still many thousands of contents stored in the Time Capsules remaining and needing attention. With few exceptions we have found the content disturbing.

There are times when we are obliged to pay attention to the many other developments in our peoples' environments. Although the vast majority of the needs and life enhancing systems we have developed and manufactured during many centuries are working to near-perfection, consideration must be paid at all times to potential lessening of the highest standards in every minute aspect of our society's construction.

There has been much confusion at the latest content of one of the small evidences, found in one Time Capsule, labelled 'Lifestyle'. This addressed the importance given to the presentation of personal appearances. Many individuals, of all ages, seem to find it necessary to smear their skin with various mixtures and colours. Much time was spent on this and many hours wasted making decisions as to individual preferences. Once again we ask ourselves why this is deemed to be so popular and come to the conclusion that it is, once again, based on the commodity named as Money.

We still find it absurd that so much emphasis is given to this item consisting of bits of plastic and circles of metal with the name of Money. The Area Leaders guarantee that all needs are met fairly and sufficiently and no individual lacks in any area of development.

In the twenty and twenty-first centuries even head hair was given this concentrated attention. We have learned about this and eliminated it. All peoples have growth of an acceptable amount of body hair. There is also no need for our peoples to paint their finger and toenails for possibly the same reason as the attention paid to other parts of the body. We have instructed our peoples that there are priorities and individuals spending time on decorating themselves is not something we encourage. We have noted from the evidence in the Time Capsules that there can be negative outcomes if an individual feels not able to function unless there are artificial additions. Personal appearances appear to have caused much unhappiness in the young.

After fulfilling many of the mandatory duties required from the position of Area Leaders we found an enthusiasm growing to further our investigations into the Time Capsule contents. Our reactions varied from disgust to admiration.

One of the capsules was labelled 'Space' and we were enthusiastic in anticipating the contents.

In the year 1969, there was the first landing on our moonplanet. This was a unique event and not repeated for at least half a century. Watching men in strange white suits walking on the surface of what we consider to be a subsidiary of our earth was of interest to us as we cannot grasp why this was undertaken during the time of great global strife and poverty. This Money that was so vital to the structure of the past was spent in huge amounts to reach our moonplanet before any other area of the world. It was an American continent that won the pointless race. There followed a vacuum of achievement and no improvement in the overall living standards or peacefulness for many centuries.

Our Area Leaders are confident that all the errors of past centuries have been, and still are, a valuable source of information to enable us to avoid similar catastrophes. Our intensity, when investigating the past millennia, has grown as we are increasingly aware that there must be no repetition.

We again open the Time Capsule with the title 'Lifestyle'.

We see a multitude of peoples with pictures on their skin. Legs, arms, torsos and even faces covered with dark ugly lines of strange images. We wonder why these peoples felt the need for mundane activities. These strange skin patterns are named as 'tattoos'. These are complicated pictures permanently printed by sharp, thin implements into the skin.

The pictures change to people having treatments to their hair. Acquiring different colours appear to be of great importance. Money was exchanged for this. Clothing was also of great importance to these peoples and many differing types were apparently essential.

We produce our clothing from resources which are recyclable and users can choose from appropriate styles according to their occupation. Very little attention is given to any colours or unnecessary details. There are more essential activities that take precedence. Our peoples have no need to spend valuable time engaging in activities with no positive and productive outcomes. They have many vital engagements to undertake, closely supervised and monitored, guaranteeing perfect results.

In another small part of the content of a Time Capsule, there is evidence of all the words spoken during the time that the peoples' representatives attended the Houses of Parliament. We have found many records of these buildings, which were totally destroyed many centuries before time present.

We have such an abundance of material we have decided to look at a small portion at each session as we are finding all the stimulation taking an increasing amount of our valuable time.

As the contents referring to the leaders overseeing control of the peoples of three millennia time past were very complicated to us, we limited the time as previously agreed.

However, a record of all communications within this Houses of Parliament building were of a particular interest to us.

One item referred to a discussion about the production of weapons of mass destruction which were then sold to other parts of the world for this money commodity. Some representatives became agitated and spoke of the lack of moral judgement in providing these weapons, which were used to kill and maim enemies. The text indicates that many civilians were destroyed. Once again, this money commodity resulted in what we would consider poor judgement. This is another area we have almost totally controlled, and are making enormous progression towards ensuring a level of confidence throughout the landmasses without resorting to negotiation or persuasion for the overwhelming majority.

As we continue to learn from the idiocy of the past generations it has given us increased energy to ensure we learn from the mistakes. We are growing in confidence in the awareness that our systems are producing the pre-determined results.

With an increasing regularity our Area Leaders devote time and energy to maintaining innovative and consistent research into all defence procedures and standards. We know there are further explorations of more intricate details which are permanently under scrutiny and which will receive the Area Leaders full attention when appropriate.

It was decided that the maximum effort into the defence mechanisms had been achieved and therefore research into another Time Capsule instigated. Once again the capsule was entitled 'Environment' with the time past dating record of 2000.

We watched as a particularly bewildering scene showed large areas covered with red flowers. There was a product from these that was made into another named as 'drugs'. They were taken by mouth, injected into the body by a needle, sniffed or added to liquid. They were very popular. There was no information given to us as to the reasons for this behaviour and we assume it was these substances, when sold, for this ubiquitous Money commodity, stimulated the involvement. We have developed the definite opinion that the providers, receiving Money, was the cause of much unhappiness. The information we managed to gain from this capsule was limited and therefore, as we have no use for it, we decided not to undertake any further research.

During another session we found evidence of another pointless occupation. This involved setting fire to a small tube of something named as tobacco and breathing it into the lungs. We are sometimes overcome by the apparent lack of guidance given to the peoples in what appear to be useless activities. We have developed a certain level of sympathy for these unfortunate Ancients. The younger Ancients appeared to have no genuine control over the lives they led.

A minority of the populations were giving attention to the urgency of the planet's survival, many of whom appeared to be the younger of the Ancients. There were some exception, as we have just researched from a new Time Capsule. All the destructive forces we had investigated were named and many intricate details given of the profound seriousness of Global Warming and Climate Change.

We had a growing respect for the very young Ancients as they tried to get their voices heard. We were impressed that many of the older Ancients had also started to join in with the increasing incidents of the protesting younger peoples. We saw images of many thousands of peoples of all ages and colours walking peacefully carrying banners on which there were signs indicating they were fully aware of the dangers facing the environment.

Many of the banners had 'EXTINCTION REBELLION' on them. We were confused when we saw many of these peaceful peoples being forced away by men in uniform. This was yet another experience that we took away with us in silence. We have the evidence that all the effort by these people did not have the desired outcome.

As we are rapidly developing our ultimately advanced and almost final robotic systems in the area of defence, the workforces are given rewards to ensure they reap the benefits from this essential protection. The Area Leaders are proud of the high level of life- security regulations achieved during the last millennium. They are confident that, by providing ecologically sound and secure living systems, the populations will exist in peace and comfort. They are, however, aware that vigilance will be needed to continue the production of all essential security items.

The Area Leaders did not admit to each other that their interest into the research of the Time Capsules was growing to such an extent that the intense attention needed to ensure all areas were functioning in an acceptable way might be compromised.

There had never been a time when they did not feel in control. The many security mechanisms in place had given them a confidence that they never previously had to doubt. They, individually, had always worked as a ubiquitous team, relying on a united ability to oversee the functioning of the security lines.

Not having any ability, or need, to communicate using words, facial expressions or physical signs, the Summiters lived in a silent, unemotional world. They had no experience of any other ways of 'living'. In this respect, their ignorance was a fact with which they all existed with indifference.

Eleven

They that have power to hurt and well do none,
That do not do the thing they most do show,
Who, moving others, are themselves as stone.
Unmoved, cold, and to temptation slow:
They rightly do inherit heaven's graces,
and husband nature's riches from expense.
They are the lords and owners of their faces,
Others but stewards of their excellence.
The summer's flower is to the summers sweet,
Though to itself it only live and die,
But if that flower with base infection meet,
The basest weed outbraves his dignity:
For sweetest things turn sourest by their deeds;
Lilies that fester smell far worse than weeds.

Sonnet 94
– William Shakespeare

Sea levels have been closely monitored and all living and working systems placed safely above any risk of waveclamp. This is another system of which the Area Leaders are confidently positive, simultaneously reiterating the need for communication between all systems and populations throughout the Worldmass.

The Area Leaders, representing the different landmasses, respond to the specific needs of each. There are difficulties which we have overcome to provide water to those increasingly sandlocked. We have found more evidence of the times of 2500 that were known to have been particularly challenging as the supplies of unpolluted water become increasingly difficult to access. In the memory vaults the history shows how the global temperature rose. We know the causes in instant time but all the statistics indicate that the peoples made little or no impetus into mitigating the causes. Much of the storage of water was inadequate and thus there was yet another crisis. Peoples were instructed to store rainwater but this became problematical as the incidence of rainfall became much less frequent. When it did occur, often at unusual seasonal times, it was of many times the usual amount and caused flooding and destruction of the earth nutrients, by rapidly washing them away. As the Ancients had no adequate sophisticated storage systems, this was another cause of overall ecological degradation.

This added to our questioning concerning the ability of the Ancients past to find solutions to obvious problems. The Earthmasses are are surrounded by salinated water, and although it has been polluted, we have found methods of treatment in our mass underground tanks to ensure adequate supply of pure water for our populations. It is apparent that very little global thought was invested in issues affecting the future populations. In contrast, our principles are based on protecting, improving and controlling all that is needed for a positive environment.

The records show that there were many mammals in the old Worldmasses used to provide food. These were classified as animals and kept in large buildings. They were sometimes seen outside eating the earth lining which appears to be a green colour. We have reports indicating that these animals produced a liquid named milk which was used to give sustenance to the populations. The same report indicated that these animals chewed the green leaf and gave off toxic fumes which caused much irreversible disturbance of the essential levels in the ecological systems. We cannot be certain of this but it must be one of the causes of the decline of most of the populations at that time although we know there must have been other events.

The researchers, when further investigating the contents of the Time Capsules, were once again confronted by the item called 'Money'. It was constantly occurring in all areas of the time Capsule's contents.

This is not a fact we can comprehend immediately. These small plastic sheets represented a certain value of exchange and tiny metal discs were transferred from one person to another for services or articles. This all appears very unnecessary and a cause of apparent discontent leading to much inequality and resentment. There was a minority of peoples owning much of this 'Money' and possessions resulting in societies of individuals grouping together and trying to emulate those with fortune. We cannot understand the logicality of this. We have, therefore, eliminated this negativity and guarantee all our peoples have the basic needs addressed. We were proud to announce, recently, another achievement of immense importance. The advanced robotic defence shields are now installed in almost every area. Only a minimal number of peoples are outside the totally controlled systems. The Area Leaders are aware that this needs continuous and vigilant monitoring but are increasingly confident that we have the knowledge to oversee any situation not conducive to our expectations. We feel we have almost reached a pinnacle of advanced surveillance. We are, however, in the knowledge of a residue of ominous, and often difficult to identify, small clans hidden within populations. We are becoming increasingly in possession of the knowledge that, because of an atmosphere of silence, our robotic instant information delivery must be at the level of perfection that we demand. We are increasingly suspicious that these clans might be hidden in obscure parts of the Earthmass.

> *"I found the poems in the fields,*
> *And only wrote them down."*

> – John Clare

We, the Area Leaders, consistently communicate with each other and ensure the appropriate robots are employed to identify any signs of threat to our mutual ambitions. Information has been collected robotically of unnamed categories we appear unable to access; the reasons for this is increasingly frustrating, but the Area Leaders are all working together, receiving and transmitting information in immediate time, the intention of which is to prevent any discordant actions from what must be very few remote peoples.

We have the surveillance robots currently travelling along the inspection wires throughout these remote areas. In time immediate, there is evidence of certain creations of intense energy clusters. We are increasing the Area Leaders' interactions in these suspected lands.

Our Worldmass populations are at a critical stage in the overall plan and no event will be permitted to cause interruption. These robotic surveillance systems will ensure all the plans will and must succeed.

We have decided to leave a space for a renovation of the Area Leaders. The time is appropriate for the substitution of many. Research has been positive but we are with the knowledge that the Area Leaders have achieved their maximum output and will be replaced automatically. This is accomplished with no reactive effects and consistent research in all categories of our needs will continue.

The new Area Leaders from one of the outer zones have their Time Capsule research allocation and, once again, see a mysterious occupation that causes concern.

There were images of very graceful animals, with a person on the back. The animals had what appeared to be metal bars through their mouths. There seemed to be metal curves on their feet. The person had straps attached to the metal mouth bars to, presumably, guide the animal.

We did not comprehend the action that followed. The animals, with the person on its back, were made to jump over high barriers. This, once again, was inexplicable to us. We watched as the populations watching got very active and noisy. There were animals that fell. This was uncomfortable for us to watch. If there had been these beautiful animals in time immediate, we would treasure them and treat them with kindness. We suspected that this was another interpretation of the word 'race' and noticed that 'Money' was, once again, passing between peoples.

One very challenging outcome of this activity was the destruction of these fallen animals. A man with a weapon killed the beautiful creatures that had fallen and which were obviously of no further use. We decided to eliminate these records as they would have no purpose in our future. This is yet another activity that appears to have no positive outcome. We communicated all this information to the other Area Leaders.

Twelve

Fall leaves, fall; die flowers away;
Lengthen night and shorten day;
Every leaf speaks bliss to me,
Fluttering from the Autumn tree.

I shall smile when wreaths of snow
Blossom where the rose should grow;
I shall sing when night's decay
Ushers in a drearier day.

'Fall, Leaves, fall'
– Emily Bronte

Another Area Leader group's research is into a vital item of concern; one of which we are of the opinion that we have made the correct decisions in respect of our elderly populations. This was also the time present decision to replace some redundant Area Leaders.

There is a time when a certain type of tiredness is experienced, especially when the individual has reached the age which intensive research and investigations can cause fatigue. This is when the person volunteers for a pre-extinction analysis system. Our robots are programmed to perform all that is necessary to ensure the individual's needs are completely met with kindness and dignity. Thus there is an elimination of life. There are no circumstances resulting in an individual's requirements not being met. As the decision to eliminate life is made, the robotic receiver can energise the procedure when given the instruction. The subsequent time is spent productively as the remnants of the individual will contain much valuable genetic material that will benefit insertion into our newest additions to the populations. We are confident that the tranquil response from those of our populations at the end of productive life indicates the correct action has been taken.

We opened a Time Capsule named 'Care of the Elderly'. We have been researching how the elderly populations were managed in the time of the Ancients. There appear to be very large buildings with many sleeping areas in which the old are installed. There appear to be many illnesses from which these people suffer and there seems to be very little effort to remove them from these buildings. We are relieved that we do not have the sicknesses that the Ancients seem to acquire from what appears to be a young age.

There was also evidence of these elderly peoples being given many substances. We judged this was to alleviate their illnesses.

They also seemed to be left with no attention for an extended length of time. No movement or exercise of the body was encouraged and many had an expression of detachment. When an Ancient was at the end of life, they were placed in a box and frequently burnt. Looking at the ceremony that surrounded this procedure, there seemed to be a minimum of concern about the remains. We ensure that all useful parts of the body are kept for research and, if needed, conserved for future inclusions.

Some of the Ancients were buried in vast parts of green land. As these no longer exist we are inquisitive as to their position in time present. However, we do not intend to investigate this as it is felt that the outcome would once again be negative. There are scenes of many elderly individuals sitting in chairs looking at large screens without appearing to show any responses. Some of these people are placed in what were named 'Residential Homes' or, if much 'Money' was exchanged, 'Nursing Homes'. Workers travelled from many landmasses to help in these homes but there were very poor facilities for their training. The workers were given very little 'Money' for the devotion they gave to the many elderly people. We have specific robots to help carers function appropriately in responding to the needs of the elderly. The Area Leaders learned that there was much concern over the lack of facilities for those Ancient peoples at the final years of their lives. We, ourselves, have learnt that people have needs at different ages and respond accordingly with help from our robotic agencies. Repeatedly, we ask why no action was taken by the Ancients to alleviate the problem.

We now have allocated time when all events are powered by our robotic systems. This is an achievement which is closely monitored as an awareness has been stimulated in part by the contents of the Time Capsules. The allocated time of robotic involvement is closely monitored to ensure our peoples have their own engagement in productive activity. We have learnt that robotic involvement is essential but not to the disadvantage of the ability of our peoples to engage in acceptable activities with positive outcomes.

Thirteen

This living hand – now warm and capable
Of earnest grasping, would, if it were cold
And in the icy silence of the tomb,
So haunt thy days and chill thy dreaming nights
That thou wouldst wish thine own heart dry of blood
So in my veins red life might stream again,
And thou be conscience- calmed – see here it is—
I hold it towards you.

'To fanny Browne'
– John Keats

We have decided to open a Time Capsule named as 'Internet'. We pride ourselves on our sophisticated interactive method of communication. It has been noted that the attention to screens of differing sizes was, in our observation, the symptom of many of the difficulties in behaviour manifested by the Ancients. We have learnt that screens can cause obsessive reactions. We have made decisions to limit the use to essential learning.

The Ancients' records in our possession indicate many instances of numbers of peoples involved in negative activities increasing to an unacceptable level. It has become apparent that there was much 'Money' involved in this. One statistic we have noted, in the year 2018, over 4000 of the peoples, in one landmass alone, were killed by misuse of drugs. To us it stimulates the frequently asked question, 'Why?' We suspect the 'Money' item is involved yet again, but are convinced this is only part of a much deeper problem.

It is apparent that 'drugs' make the user feel detached and more able to address the reasons for taking them. We have researched more into this subject and it has become clear to us that there are certain categories of the populations that are most involved. We have found more statistics indicating that the very poor, homeless and 'ex-servicemen' are the most at risk. We have difficulty in understanding the role of the last named.

The ubiquitous 'Money' item, named frequently, is exchanged for the provision of 'drugs'. We are increasingly determined to disconnect with any possible reasons in the future for the need of this item. Once again the Area Leaders allow themselves to access the facility named as 'The Internet' in order to eradicate any damaging content. We need to be aware of this to ensure we utilise the information.

As we watch a small proportion of the immense content of this 'Internet', we are increasingly aware of how much negative effect it had on the populations. We were affected by the amount of time the very young Ancients were staring at scenes of nudity, violence and other negative examples. We do not have an understanding of the need the young Ancients had for this type of occupation. We, the Area Leaders, ensure there are numerous permitted activities for the varying stages of development.

There is much apprehension within all the Area Leaders

groups concerning the damaging contents of the Time Capsules. Our robotic systems will powerfully control all that is necessary to ensure we are not affected. After a short time, the research will continue, but for time present, the Area Leaders have decided to curtail all investigations. We will guarantee that the ensuing time will be spent productively. We have a continuing intention to ensure all our systems in each of the developmental landmasses have maintained the optimum level of advancement with sophisticated security.

We have become increasingly aware that the time spent on researching the Time Capsules has produced a potentially negative outcome within us which we cannot allow to continue. Therefore we are ensuring time will be spent on intensifying our standards of functioning. We are confident this is the correct procedure.

Some considerable time passed until the Area Leaders reached reached a point at which they felt able to continue with the research into the contents of the Time Capsules.

One specific subject that seems to occur with increasing intensity was contained in a Time Capsule named as 'Mental Health'. We do not comprehend the translation of this into our life-skills. However, we want to investigate this subject as the information might be useful.

There are statistics relating to the number of people suffering from an affliction named as 'depression'. This is an illness of which we have no experience so we will learn from it. It appears this affliction makes the person unable to function positively. There was an increasing number of all ages of Ancients affected.

One aspect of the general life-skill conditions provided by the Ancient leaders appears to be the lack of investigation into the reasons causing the increasing number of very young people suffering from this. We pride ourselves in our ability to anticipate and prevent any possible negative outcomes for our young peoples. All young are monitored and occupied, from birth to the end of their life. All development is nurtured by those with experience of the most productive personal growth programmes, both mentally and physically. In time present we have pride in the attainments of our Worldmass peoples. We also find ourselves grateful for the research resulting from the Time Capsules. There are, simultaneously, rejections of neglectful actions taken by those able to make decisions on behalf of the Ancients.

To grant ourselves a brief respite from the devastating content of so many of the Time Capsule contents, we opened one named as 'Supermarkets'. This title intrigued us and the Area Leaders from the Oceana Area joined the investigation. Once again we were puzzled by the intensity of the movements of the peoples. The faces were, once again, dull.

We learnt a 'Supermarket' was the provider of sustenance for the peoples. It was a large building with rows of shelves filled with foods, all of which are alien to us. People had containers on wheels which were used for putting the chosen foods in. Once again, 'Money' was involved. This commodity was exchanged for the items chosen in the trolley and taken out again to place on a moving shelf so that each item can be scanned with another machine and the cost totalled. This was all explained to us and we were perplexed as the items were placed in bags for the customer to take to the method of transport, presumably to take to the place of living, then taken from the transporter to the place of storage. To us this seems a total waste of time and effort.

We were overcome with the need to make the strange throat noise. This was unusual for us but quite pleasant and relaxing. We knew the Ancients frequently experienced something named as 'laughing' and decided to investigate this action further to enable us to utilise the experience.

Having spent much time ensuring all the security systems were working at maximum capacity we were positively anticipating the following Time Capsule research.

In pursuit of this decision we opened a Time Capsule named as 'Comedians'. The Area Leaders from the Open Desert areas were chosen to experience this category. The scene contained a large area with rows of peoples watching one person on a platform talking to them. The people were open-mouthed and showing the 'laughing' activity. We did not understand the sounds coming from the large mouth of the person on the platform. We were affected by the 'laughing' coming from the spectators and found ourselves joining in reluctantly, making strange gurgling noises. We didn't know the reason why we were joining in with the 'laughter'. We were not in a comfortable state and, as a unit, curtailed the experience.

After some period of time it was decided to open yet another Time Capsule. The Area Leaders have shared all the information learned from the Capsules up to the time present and found a Capsule named as 'The Examination System'. This was an unfamiliar word so we were interested to understand the implications.

In many centuries past, before the destruction, all the very young Ancients were forced to undergo a series of 'Examinations'. These were systems of tests that the individual undertook to be judged as to the suitability of further study. This was very strange to us. We wondered what happened to those not succeeding. No information appeared to be on the records.

Fourteen

This time of suspicion, enclosed in the dark.
With wind in the trees and floods on the roads,
Up with the owl and down with the lark,
The inhabited mind rejecting the load.

The Area Leaders decided to investigate further and opened the Time Capsule named 'Education and Schools- Year 2000'. We had no previous facts about this and were slightly apprehensive.

The Time Capsule indicated all small Ancients attended school in the rich countries. Some cost 'Money' and were named as 'Private'. We had no experience of this word. It appeared as an awkward system of division. Why should this happen? This soon became clear. People with 'Money' in the rich countries, could send their small ones to these 'Private 'schools. The majority of the small ones attended what were named as 'State Schools'. This is very confusing for us. In a similar way as 'Religion' this results in individuals being separated from their similar aged populations. We decided to continue with this research. At an older age, this attitude was repeated. Some older Ancients were separated from their peers and received their education in another building. We think this would result in, once again, division between the young peoples that need to cooperate with each other. Therefore, as they mature, they will not have an understanding of the needs of all others of a similar age.

It reminded us of the attitudes, in millennia past, to the non-white peoples by some of the whites of the population. We have come to the obvious conclusion that it would be of benefit if all white peoples turned black overnight and the black peoples woke up with white skin. We are convinced attitudes would have changed extremely rapidly.

We are of the opinion that our evolutionary genetic transformations have obliterated the historical unnatural segregations of our peoples.

All our populations, eventually, will have identical physical constituents. We are optimistic that we have nearly attained this outcome. The Area Leaders find, when comparing their own decisions with those of the Ancients, a satisfaction that their own are completely correct.

It was almost by accident that they came across details of the section of the peoples that owned enough of the 'Money' to spend it on an education that completely divided their young from the majority. Some of these segregated Learners were sent to 'boarding schools'. We approve of this concentrated attention but only if this facility is undertaken by all. It appears that these 'boarders' actually lived at these schools during the time they were learning and then proceeded to 'University'. These were magnificent buildings of which we have few remaining records. It was of some interest to us to see a small amount of evidence of the few historic edifices; most were destroyed many centuries in time past. The buildings were indeed wonderful creations, as were many of the temples and cathedrals, none of which remain intact.

The records contained in the Time Capsules emphasise the importance of vigilance. The Ancients' Leaders must have lost control of the peoples at some time long past. We looked with admiration at the intricate architectural details of the few remaining visual records.

The individual Area Leaders in each small or vast land-mass have total communication systems. As each stage of development or research is undertaken the information is transmitted by the numerous advanced robotic connections and all required knowledge is transferred. This system is virtually immediate and all decisions agreed unanimously before final outcomes.

The Area Leaders needed to spend some of the time present to, once again, guarantee the security systems were working to maximum capacity.

The Area Leaders were responsible for the transportations of the next section of the peoples as Moonmass residents. This was robotically achieved and no adverse situations occurred.

The time taken to travel between the planets is efficient, energy compliant and ultimately very pleasing. We have no incidents of failure and the Moonmass residents who are allocated time on another planet immediately take up positions of responsibility.

There has been some time lapse before the Area Leaders next visit to the Time Capsules. All areas have been reassessing the impact of the upgraded robotic security systems. We have gained further knowledge of an unknown concentration of unidentifiable energy, once again in remote areas of the land-mass. We are installing additional and continuous monitoring robots in all the suspected areas. This has taken time.

The Area Leaders are increasingly enthusiastic to return to the Time Capsules. The Highland Leaders take on the responsibility. The chosen Capsule contained information once again, named 'The Internet'. We appreciated the title as we translated it to mean 'connections between'.

The content of this Capsule was immense and it was decided to limit the involvement.

We were informed that all areas in time past had an accessible service on personal screens. There were numerous facilities and we decided to open one named 'Facebook'. Very quickly we knew this was yet another of the Ancients' failures. All the peoples were looking at the screens for many hours in a day. Many of the young were upset by vile messages and images they received. Why they didn't turn the machine off was inexplicable to us. Where were the guiding and supervising older Ancients? Why were they not monitoring this?

We found ourselves unable to terminate this activity. There were many services, but the young seemed to choose the ones that disturbed them. Messages, named as 'Tweets' could be sent to another person, or anyone in the old world, sometimes so personal and unpleasant, that any respect we had for the 'Ancients' evaporated. We know many of these young people became the victims of 'mental health' problems.

We decided to try to locate an item in the content that might give us a more positive outlook towards the Ancients. The small amount of respect we had found for them was evaporating. We managed to find items named as 'Fortnite', 'Minecraft' and other titles that appeared meaningless. None of the content made us 'laugh'.

We watched avidly and noted that three suns time had passed. We quickly terminated all systems.

The Area Leaders knew that they had become fixated.

They became aware that too much time had been spent researching the conditions of life experienced by the Ancients.

However, reasons were found for further investigations into the Time Capsules. There were many that caused an obsession and the Area Leaders found they were increasingly unable to terminate the activity.

The Area Leaders experienced a condition of agitation when they were forced to stop the involvement. Even exercise, sleep and nourishment actions were undertaken reluctantly. They were all finding excuses for spending time on various 'games' they had located in the Time Capsule.

Time passed in a fixated and silent occupation.

The security lines were neglected.

PART TWO
The Age of The Summiters

Fifteen

A blossom in its witchery of bloom,
There gathered, dwells in beauty and perfume.
The singing bird, the brook that laughs along
There ceaseless sing and never thirst for song.
A pleasing image to its page conferred
In living character and breathing word
Becomes a landscape heard and felt and seen.

from *'Shadows of Taste'*
– John Clare

Two millennia years prior to this age, an unexpected devastation had occurred and the outcomes were far worse than even the most extreme pessimist could have foreseen.

The Summiters evolved from the superior genetic living microcosm stores of the virtually extinct Area Leaders. There were few survivors and only the very strongest could overcome the conditions.

There are four categories of inhabitants , spread throughout the landmasses:

1. Starters – named instantly seconds after existence.
2. Learners – child trainees.
3. Advancers – those absorbing the necessary skills to be promoted from the Learner category.
4. Summiters – These are the oldest, most influential and powerful.

In appearance the populations have red hair and brownish skin and possess an exceptional strength.

There is no need for language as all necessary thoughts are transmitted automatically. The eyes are small and protruding, ears are tiny hollow tubes. Mouths have evolved to be the appropriate size to accept the necessary sustenance. All thoracic bones have evolved into a permanent curved formation. We know, from information learnt from the Central Brainstore Hub, many millennia past, the vertebrae in the back had been relatively straight.

There will be an explanation but, in time present, we are confident that the cause must be the type of lifestyle adopted by the Ancients.

The Summiter has wide, flat feet. Hands have three digits.

The Summiter females are almost identical to the males. They are also tall and strong with muscular frames. Breasts are absent. There is a natural merging of the sexes which has evolved with little interruption. This has not yet been completed but the result is inevitable.

At time present there is little need for replacements as the age which the individual is no longer of use is extending. We have an expectation of life well into a second century.

Development of our society has taken over two millennia.

We inherited a land of brown, black and poisonous. There was darkness and a completeness of silence.

It has taken much research and physical input from all the Summiters to work together to develop an environment within which our peoples can develop to their full capacity.

We are producing much of our present needs by constructing enormous 'sustenance' buildings in which to produce food elements. These are automatically distributed to our populations on a systematic procedure. Much of the produce is underground. We use no hormones or pesticides. Minerals returned from the planets are used.

We have much knowledge installed in the Central Brainstore Hub gathered from the populations on our planets. Their systems have given us much information. We have installed energy conservation techniques on our landmasses. There are no areas causing difficulties as the planets cooperate and rely on transportation of sustenance. After the devastation of two millennia past, there were few survivors on this planet. Only the strongest learnt to adapt. We are satisfied with the inventive systems that have evolved enabling the continuation of life. The peoples work with these established systems.

The most powerful system that has evolved is the Central Brainstore Control. This is an intense centre of advanced technological interaction.

The Central Brainstore Control has total power over every individual's thought processes and transmits these with any relevant information automatically between them in immediate time.

There is total silence between individuals. Each being has their own receptive Brainstore. An essential part of their genetic construction is that emotions are not permitted, as these would interfere in the speed of transference of information between the peoples. The Summiters generate all the considered necessary information or instruction in time immediate.

All Summiters have the respect and obedience of the populations.

Travel is swift and automated. It is obligatory for each person to visit another planet once every six months. We have made perfect selections from the populations of the planets to enhance our own genetic store. We have learnt to cross-fertilise our embryos with those of another planet and the results are expected and exceptional.

Transference to another planet takes little time as we have compacted time. On arrival this is reversed and the normal twenty hours of artificial daylight is re-established. We were fortunate to recover many skills from the few remaining superior earth remnants.

There have been many statistics that have indicated some of the causes of the damage to the environment of previous Worldmasses.

The Summiters have instantly transferred all this knowledge to the peoples to receive in their Brainstores. It is important that this knowledge is of common ownership.

Sixteen

*'Youth is the time to study wisdom, age the time to practise it.
Experience is always instructive, I admit, but it is only useful
in the time we have left to live.'*

'Reveries of the Solitary Walker'
– Jean-Jacques Rousseau

Gradually, the expertise has developed into our present
peaceful and contented living situations. The many robotic
systems that have been developed during the last millennia
have resulted in the creation of complete zones of equality. These are overseen by Summiters which are the highest
grade of peoples. The development of Brainstores enabling
all peoples instant understanding and knowledge of all necessary sections of information is proceeding at the predetermined rate.

We are producing much of the present needs by farm-
ing mainly underground. The light and energy sources are
stimulated by stored solar energy. We have much to do as
research indicates there is probably an even more efficient
method of manufacturing the elements needed to sustain
the population. We have many thousands of researchers

around the Earth, Moon and Marsmasses. Our Central Brainstore Hubs facilitate instant connections throughout all the research areas and the Summiters are satisfied that, in a few hundred years, the populations will be totally self- sustainable.

Another area of which the Summiters have developed is the total cessation of aggression between areas. To achieve this has taken many centuries. The Central Brainstore Hub had transferred the information in respect of numerous wars in past time. We are in the possession of the knowledge that war is unacceptable.

There are strict laws against any threatening actions from one area against another and we are hopeful progress will accelerate to achieve imminent total world peace. We do not allow any waste of life and time.

We have gained the knowledge that to possess weapons causes competition and a need to destroy others who might be seen as threats. It has taken many centuries of intense research and application to reach the levels of time present existence. We will not allow any repetition of errors past. As the Summiters live for a minimum of two centuries, the need for replacements only happens infrequently. A vintage Summiter is aware of the exact time to self-destruct and will trigger this independently. The residue of the Summiter is processed for research. A replacement is put in place and is a smooth and straightforward procedure.

We have encouraged a passive and accepting attitude from our populations. This is now endemic and we have a total absence of non-cooperation.

We have research and systematic investigations in progress at all times. There are always projected aims which we always address as they occur. As we have instant guidance from the Central Brainstore Hub, there are minimal instances needing urgent attention. Light and energy sources are accessed from stored solar satellites. These are self-functioning plates absorbing the power needed to activate all essential light, movement and heat. We have many thousands of researchers situated around the Earth, Moon and Marsmasses. Our instant Brainstore hubs facilitate immediate connections.

The Summiters are in possession of the facts concerning any potential aggression between Worldmass areas. We suspect this was the cause of the destructions in the years 2050 and 4000. We have strict laws against any threats from one landmass against another and we are hopeful that progress will avoid the errors of the past. If aggression is reported, instant treatment is prescribed by the specific landmass hub. Bombs, weapons of mass destruction, chemical weapons, missiles, drones, guns, bullets, knives, clubs and bows and arrows have been eliminated. We are proud that there is an instant recognition by the Brainstore hubs of any item considered as a potential weapon. These have all been destroyed and any movements of populations suspected of manufacturing these items immediately addressed.

Instant annihilation of the instigator and any potential war items is then achieved. All landmasses have the knowledge of this rule and know of the response if it is disobeyed.

We will not permit the waste of so many millions of lives by one part of the landmass trying to destroy another. This is a pointless exercise and our first target many centuries in time past was for Worldmass peace.

We have records imparting the information of outcomes of the numerous areas of aggression in time past resulting in loss of innocent populations of all ages. Our present systems of instant safety procedures has resulted in Worldmass peace for a considerable time.

We are constantly researching how we can develop a perfect lifestyle for our populations. With this as our aim we provide water exercise for all our peoples. Our water storage and purification units are available throughout the landmasses. We need peoples of a strong and fit stature and moving within water has proved to be beneficial in this respect. The constant research undertaken by our peoples demand a high level of energy output.

Starters are enrolled into the water programme immediately after they reach acceptable size. This can be from birth as the systems of procreation we employ are reaching optimum levels of perfection. There is compulsory attendance by all population members.

In our silent environment, emotional reactions are unnecessary. All Brainstores are controlled and solitary existence is maintained for the majority of the time.

The Summiters from the Africanical zone have recently found very strange materials. With the techniques they have developed over many centuries they now have access to information from two to four millennia past.

During excavations to construct further living facilities for the proposed future Starters, there was a discovery which caused the Central Brainstore an overactive stimulation. This was unacceptable to the Summiters and it took some prolonged connection to the Central Brainstore Control to enable them to proceed in examining the contents of the massive containers. It was accepted that their Brainstore knowledge of these must not come into contact with any other sections of their populations. Only the Summiters would be permitted access.

The Summiters were committed to use any of the content as a guidance to their future Brainstore development but only if relevant and of use. All this material was over four millennia years past left by peoples at the suspected decline of their existence.

All the items were alien to the experience of the Summiters, therefore all have been entered into the Central Brainstore Hub facilities for automatic construction to give them the instant knowledge and understanding of the content.

The Summiters have the information that these peoples of four millennia past were identified as Ancients by the peoples who eventually succeeded them. All subsequent harvesting will be of intense secrecy. The Summiters were the only peoples having viewpoints of the methods by which the Ancients functioned. It was obviously essential that their complete peacefulness was maintained and any risk of donating non-useful facts to their populations automatically destroyed.

The Summiters were representatives of each Earthmass zone. They communicated by instant brain contact, words being redundant millennia past. Transmitting between the Summiters from the other zones was essential to ensure they were the only section of the population to own it.

The Summiters think it is vital to look at the history from at least four millennia past for future reference. Its importance was becoming increasingly clear. As there are many other areas of progress needing our attention, some time will pass before we intend investigating the immense contents of the containers.

One of the many areas of our research concerns the final investigation into meteorites, of which there are a considerable number. These are easily located by our advanced infrasound systems. We are in the process of utilising the energy as we alter the orbits of the meteorites to our space storage cylinders. This energy, produced by the meteorites, is of numberless proportions and we are confident that our populations will profit subsequently in many positive forms.

It is possible information relevant to the increase in our zone temperatures might be stored within the containers and we intend to investigate this.

There is a slight delay in ordering a Summiter team to proceed in their investigations and The Central Brainstore Control Hub uses the artificial intelligence core to its maximum potential before permitting the first Summiter to access to the containers.

The Opening of The Containers.

At a time considered appropriate, a group from Area One were instructed to investigate the contents of the containers as a team. They were given complete and relevant information about the procedure. The Brainstore Control Hub automatically enabled the Summiters immediate visual Brainstore access.

The Summiter team entered the container and were given access to a disc which automatically entered their Brainstores.They received images simultaneously, giving information of the extinct peoples of the years from 2000.

In the years 2000 to 3000 peoples looked different from the Summiters. Individuals had large orifices named as mouths from which items named as 'words' were emitted. These 'words' were needed so that communication could be undertaken. This is a redundant facility for us and we have no use for it.

It was noted that most of the words were not coming from the mouths but transmitted from different sized machines. These machines were used as a substitute for using words. Our present systems have superseded the necessity for this type of basic technology. The Summiters learned that four millennia past time was known as the Technological Age. All the visual images were of peoples from the youngest upwards looking down whilst holding a screen. There appeared to be many different types of screens. When we asked for more knowledge the Brainstore Control Hub informed us that the bent upper bodies were a development from life actions but, within the last two centuries, gradual straightening has evolved. No other reason was given.

The Summiters learned that many of the peoples were totally dependent on various sizes of screen. They had very large hearing mechanisms called ears and seeing sense organs called eyes, which our present populations possess. Ours are substantially smaller. Many of the Ancients had lenses in frames and their sight was substandard. Our populations have eyes that are fixed open in their heads. To look from side to side it is necessary to turn our whole bodies.

It has become obvious that the Summiter's factual comprehension and retaining skills are considerably more efficient than those of the peoples of four millennia past. The logical reason for this is transmitted from a pre-determination of stored knowledge by the Central Brainstore Control Hub.

The Summiters absorb the information about the life-habits and environments of four millennia past and learn many facts. As we are at the first impact of this we know we cannot allow any repetition of the lack of Brainstore use shown by the decisions made by the Ancients of the distant past.

Seventeen

Moonlight and dew-drenched blossom, and the scent
Of summer gardens;these can bring you all
Those dreams that in the starlit silence fall:
Sweet songs are full of odours.
                                    While I went
Last night in drizzling dusk along a lane,
I passes a squalid farm; from byre and midden
Came the rank smell that brought me once again
A dream of war that in the past was hidden.

from *'The Dream'*
– Siegfried Sassoon

Another time allocation for investigating the first container was taken by The Summiters from Area One. They worked fast and much information was instantly transferred for future investigation, storage and possible destruction.

Some paper articles were found, inside hard covers. Opening them was initially extraordinary and unknown. Of course the Summiters achieved this by not becoming emotionally excited, absorbing all the information on a theoretical level and any emotional reaction eliminated by the Central Brainstore Hub.

There were many thin layers covered in some sort of script, sometimes with drawings, indicating that these articles were highly prized as much work was involved. The Summiters, of course, have thought processes to impart anything of this sort and have no need of any materials such as they had seen. Accessing the required Brainstore channels the Summiters learned that these things were named as 'Books'. They were small and usually rectangular and their use was for an occupation named as 'Reading'.

This information was received and further knowledge was accepted to inform us that reading was an activity of decoding something named as 'print' or 'script', on the pages of the books. All these functions were achieved and retained in the Summiters' Brainstores automatically. The print, after it was decoded by the individual reading it, imparted information which was 'enjoyed' most of the time by the reader. We do not have the ability to 'enjoy' and do not have the need of it. All our requirements are met by instant transference from the Central Brainstore Hub.

The Summiters were given knowledge of many tiny silver discs and memory sticks that contained vast information about the populations of millennia past, the content of which were instantly accessible by the transference of datastreams into every Summiter's Brainstore.

Four thousand years past little humans equivalent to our Starters were seen staring at screens and total populations could be seen with their heads down staring at similar hand-held items. All our Starters have time tags inserted at birth designed to react at a specific age to ensure the development follows the prescribed calendar. Screens are unnecessary.

Continuing to assess the information within one disc, rare images were received; images of bare land of brown and black with an absence of anything moving. There was a silent darkness and images alien to us. There were black, static shapes. The Summiters learned these were different creatures, lying motionless.

They identified an isolated shape that vaguely resembled themselves and were given the information it was a man doing something named as 'talking'. The very large mouth was moving. All this was new to the Summiters and they were only permitted to watch for short sections of time. All this activity was completed in total silence.

Secrecy and silence was the usual way of behaving by all the populations and any initial or independent thoughts of uncertainty alien to them.

Further investigations resulted in the Central Brainstore Hub facilities suddenly and automatically shutting down.

There were many other actions necessary for the Summiters to enact that were not connected to the research into the containers. The Central Brainstore Hub distributed instructions simultaneously to all Summiters overseeing their areas of population. When all these duties were fulfilled, only then were they expected to complete further research into the Ancients.

The Summiters were instructed to ration themselves to a short period of session time with only one Summiter investigating the contents of one disc from one container. This was unanimously decided on, based on the instruction from The Central Brainstore Control.

This programme worked successfully of course as the Summiters had no feelings of jealousy or competitiveness. They took it in turns and their findings were simultaneously transmitted and received to the other Summiters when their session was complete.

At random Summiters were allocated an identification label. There were no choices available and therefore no dissent. The Central Brainstore Hub had the store of these labels from millennia past.

Summiter Stone was given the instruction to attend the containers for the purpose of investigating the contents. This was controlled totally and and Summiter Stone found himself at the opening of the container.

One finding was automatically relayed by Summiter Stone. He found the microscopic circular disc which he entered into his Brainstore. Immediately there were images relayed into his receptor. He could see many Learners of past millennia, all together, in an area looking at a large screen. The faces had passivity on them. This was familiar to the Summiters. The Learners seemed to be doing what their name implied.

The image then moved to a green area and the Learners had changed into different clothing and had a small globe which they were kicking around. Summiter Stone knew all these facts would be transferred to the other Summiters automatically. He was given the information that the Brainstore might cut out if he became too interested, so curtailed the activity. He was unusually fatigued for some reason and triggered his autopickup switch in his arm.

Summiter Opal was the next to have her turn. She decided to continue with the prescribed little circular discs and was absorbed by the Ancients' Learners in water. This was something she instantly understood as all the present Learners are in water every day. There seemed to be quite a lot of jumping off boards into the water, which was strange as there appeared to be no purpose. She accepted this action as fact and was impassive as required.

There was a large person with a very large mouth which was opening and closing at frequent intervals. Summiter Opal found herself becoming slightly interested and the activity was terminated. She accepted this immediately as she had felt something unusual happening in her own Brainstore. This was an unknown experience.

Summiter Bone was the next to have a session and he followed the preceding Summiters. They had all received the information from the previous sessions. Summiter Bone had noticed that Summiter Opal had not been allocated a session with the contents of one of the containers and had not received instruction to take her turn.

This fact had no feeling attached to it and was an irrelevancy and immediately discarded.

Summiter Bone followed the same pattern. This time he identified a different type of microscopic disc. He immediately received the images of a woman with something sharp. She was doing something to her arm and red liquid was coming from it. The information he received was that she was cutting her arm. Then another young man, about the same size as an Advancer, sniffing something up his nose, then losing his balance. There followed many images of the Ancient peoples' faces changing shape. Something seemed to be coming from their mouths. The information given to this action was named as vomiting.

Summiter Bone stopped, knowing this knowledge would be passed to all the other Summiters, and used as a warning. He also found himself terminated from the activity as his passivity level was not of complete perfection. He was impassive and followed the received instructions to attend to his other duties.

Eventually, Summiter Opal was instructed to continue researching into another container disc. She found herself with weird energies in her Brainstore and knew she was being constantly assessed and monitored to ensure there were no unacceptable reactions. She found herself staring at the container and being unable to make an immediate decision on what to investigate. She was overruled by the Brainstore Control Hub immediately so picked up the nearest item.

Looking at the images had an unpleasant effect on her. This was controlled by the Central Brainstore Hub and she instantly became detached. She had seen people very closely joined, wriggling and squirming. A female opened her mouth and the male hit her. This was as much as she was permitted to watch. The Central Brainstore Hub had taken control of her reactions but she was left with an uneasiness. She knew the other Summiters would have been given the same images. Returning to the group she was met with the normal controlled passive acceptance. Within herself there was a residue of something for which she had no name. She knew she wanted more information about what she had just seen.

There was an unacceptable production of a particular energy in Opal's Brainstore. This resulted in her being given different duties by the Central Brainstore Hub with immediate effect.

Eventually, after many moons, she was given another session; one she anticipated. She had received much information automatically and in immediate time from the Central Brainstore Hub that seemed to form a pattern. Any emotional reaction would be systematically inactivated. Summiter Opal would have no control.

Eighteen

As other Summiters had their dictated time within the container, each transmitting the information to the others, Summiter Opal found she was anticipating her next experience. When she was allocated this, and initiated the receptors in her own Brainstore from a miniscule memory stick, she found herself mesmerized by the content.

There was an enormous domed building, full of people. They were all wearing ornate clothing. A man in a golden cloak walked slowly up the middle of the inside of the building. He carried a large cross- shaped piece of gold. Then there was a fireball and destruction.

Opal was given knowledge about what was happening and the Central Brainstore Hub imprinted the answers. The domed building was a cathedral. The people were worshippers of a man called God and other people worshipped in other buildings called temples or churches. It was called religion. The explosion was a bomb ignited by another religion trying to destroy it.

Summiter Opal felt numb and knew she was developing an increasing interest in the time of 4000 past so immediately curtailed the activity. She wondered how the other Summiters had received the identical knowledge and if they had felt similar thoughts as herself. Nothing was transmitted to her and she managed to act detached as was expected. She was anticipating to be terminated from the task but felt an increasing sense of separation developing in her Brainstore which appeared to protect her from any censure.

There was another long interval between her container allocation and Opal discovered she was experiencing alien interferences in her functioning. She maintained her attention to all her other duties as was systematically required.

Summiter Stone had another experience to which he showed no reactions. As the scenes were transmitted to Opal she found that she could not remain detached, although she kept her whole being still and rigid, hoping the Central Brainstore Hub would overlook any signs of unacceptable emotional reactions. She was aware this was very unlikely but remained controlled, only receiving information implacably.

Summiter Opal again felt eager to personally be the initiator of more information of the years of 4000 past. She started to allow her thought processes to wander and was receptive when Summiter Bone transmitted further information. This time it related to travel. There were black surfaces on which shapes with wheels moved very slowly. There appeared to be some Ancients in these little containers. They were named as 'cars'. Then there were long, thin containers, on tracks, also moving very slowly. It must have taken a long time for the populations to get anywhere. These containers were named 'trains' the Central Brainstore informed all Summiters.

Summiter Bone's involvement must have been curtailed as his inspection of the container transmitted only a small amount of this information. Summiter Opal wondered if he might have been getting too involved with the content. She discarded this thought immediately and concentrated her energies to the expected fulfilment of her many duties. She still was inhabited with the nameless foreign energy but was, after many moons had passed, becoming accustomed to its presence. Her own Brainstore felt as though there was something unexpected in the contents, and Opal waited with some impatience for her next instruction.

It seemed as if her turn came quickly again and she found herself at the container entrance. She inserted a disc and saw people in beds, with tubes coming out of them. Other people in uniforms were sticking thin, sharp things into them. Sometimes they were given things on flat discs to put in their mouths. She was told that the place was a hospital and 4000 years past people had defects that had to be eliminated.

There was an image of a large area full of people in white coats with their mouths covered. They were replacing a person's heart with another one. This procedure was named as 'Transplanting'. That was the information that Opal's receptor stored and automatically transferred to the other Summiters. She knew that her Brainstore was experiencing some unusual reaction which could not be compared with receiving results from the research that was constantly undertaken. This could be compared with a totally complete calmness but Opal knew there was an inexplicable difference and a reason as yet unavailable to her.

She also knew that she was slowly developing an ability to block any unacceptable emotions or reactions to some of the contents of the discs but was only gradually becoming aware of the part of her Brainstore stimulating it. It was as if a distance was being created between herself and an unusual energy over which she had control. Simultaneously, she was aware that she could form a barrier between her emotions and any other recipient.

Opal wondered if the strange sensations in her Brainstore

were the signs of something unusual happening. She found herself needing reassurance that her functioning was acceptable. This was a normal procedure and one which all Summiters underwent at regular intervals. Summiter Opal had become accustomed to intense scrutiny and knew her request for monitoring was essential if she was to utilise her new found energy. She studied all the immediate expectations to reinforce her Brainstore competence. The Central Brainstore Hub accepted this request immediately. Within a nano second all her systems had been intensely inspected and her Brainstore functioning energised to its maximum capacity. There was no evidence of anything but acceptable submissive behaviour and she was temporarily relieved. However, she secreted her nucleus of a new emotional barrier awareness within herself. She became immersed in the knowledge that there was a small section of her thought processes that she could prevent another system accessing. The decision from the Central Brainstore Hub that she was in the correct functioning mode gave Opal confidence and she continued her duties with a calm knowledge that the future held something of immense importance for her.

Summiter Opal was not given a personal task of research into a container for some time but received information from the other Summiters. Most of the time she was able to remain detached as expected but one instance was exceptional.

This disc content was transmitted to her as she was completing her sustenance delivery task and she was, at first, unable to receive the facts as she almost discarded them as unbelievable.

There were trains with numerous people staggering in the road next to them. They were being pushed by other men in brown clothes with sticks and guns. There were small Ancient Starters and Learners who were occupied by 'crying'. This was defined as drops of moisture running down the face. These people were herded into the trains and were taken to what were named as Gas Chambers. Here they were killed. They had been collected from what we were told were named as Concentration Camps. These were for populations that were not acceptable. We were told there were six million of these peoples destroyed. We were not told the reason why this happened only that the Leader, named as Hitler, wanted to produce a race of super humans, so anyone that didn't match his strict expectations was destroyed.

Summiter Opal switched herself off immediately from the Central Brainstore Hub, citing fatigue. She was left with very confusing thoughts. She was aware that 'confusion' would be considered an emotional reaction and not permitted. However, no action appeared to have been taken by Central Brainstore Control. Shortly after this Summiter Bone was involved with transmitting some information from a disc which caused Summiter Opal to wonder if any of his reactions resembled her own. Perhaps they were all getting so accustomed to the contents they were finding it easier to remain negatively detached. She wondered if any of them had even the smallest feelings of emotion. She didn't risk communicating this and was careful to stimulate her newly developed ability to create her personal barrier. She knew the other Summiters' reactions had remained impassive and resistant as was deemed necessary. She would have valued and been grateful for even a small indication that there was just one other individual who could understand her own new thought processes.

When Summiter Opal next triggered the contents of a new disc, she immediately used her unique barrier mechanisms as she had ominous predictions in her Brainstore towards the contents. She knew she was successful in creating the barrier as the increasingly familiar feelings of being distant from what was happening overtook her and it was as if she was in a small, flimsy and transparent compartment separating her emotions from her permitted mechanical thoughts. The disc showed, what they had already been informed were animals, being killed.

These were pink and fat and were named as pigs. They were herded, much like the peoples from the Concentration Camps, into areas where they were killed. There was much screaming. There was roughness about the method by which these animals were taken into the killing area. This place was named as an 'Abattoir'. More information was transmitted. Apparently these pigs were going to be eaten by the populations. The images received were of the inside of the Abattoir after the pigs were hung up on hooks. There was much blood pouring out of these animals. The animals were then dissected into smaller parts and transported to other areas where they were cut into even smaller pieces. There was more travelling as large containers carried them to what were named as supermarkets. Small pieces of these pigs were wrapped in the material named as plastic and the populations visited the supermarkets to give Money in exchange for the bits of pig. There was such a concentration of information that the Central Brainstore Hub ceased to transmit. This was unprecedented.

Summiter Opal found herself wanting more information and managed to retain her apparent, but bogus, impassivity. The content of the disc she chose was almost a relief as she was expecting an experience of something which would, again, trigger an unacceptable emotion.

This time the content was much more in the areas in which the Summiters felt a familiarity. There were images of extensive, sand-covered land. There was no evidence of any movement. The temperature was 60 degrees. The Central

Brainstore Hub gave the information that nothing lived on the vast areas of land two millennia years past as a result of something named as 'Nuclear Warfare'. The Central Brainstore Hub indicated that the present populations were evolved from the remains of human life from that time. There were many facts and statistics concerning the negative choices made during time past and the disc showed the outcomes.

As Summiter Opal felt in control of her emotions she opened a disc, named as 'Climate Change', a subject that had triggered an increased interest. So much evidence was presented to her that she started to feel overwhelmed so she stimulated her anti-emotion blocking system.

There were numerous facts and incredible images of how the natural environment existed in millennia past. There were indications of the increasing dangers facing the populations. Signs that human passivity towards these dangers which would cause the eventual devastation of life as it had been known for many millions of years was increasingly obvious to Opal. She felt a deep sadness for these people. She was on the point of shutting down her receptors when something caught her attention. A list of numbers and names confronted her and she asked the Central Brainstore Hub for clarification.

All the names and numbers were the worst polluters in the year 2020. Opal studied these and retained them in her personal Brainstore. She knew these figures were of extreme importance and was increasingly interested in finding out exactly what they represented. She had the information that the words 'pollution' and 'waste' were indicators of extensive areas of neglect. She studied them and was filled with the emotion of disbelief.

Greenhouse Gas Polluters.
Areas of the World in the year 2020

Top Five	China	27.51%
	U.S.A	14.75%
	India	6.43%
	Russia	4.86%
	Japan	2.99%

Solid Waste Production

U.S.A	624 tonnes per day
China	520 tonnes per day
Brazil	149 tonnes per day
Japan	144 tonnes per day
Germany	127 tonnes per day
India	109 tonnes per day
Russia	100 tonnes per day
Mexico	99 tonnes per day
U.K	97 tonnes per day
France	90 tonnes per day

Opal asked for the definition of 'Tonnes' and received the solution as 'Unit of Mass'.

Opal knew that these figures had been recorded and stored for a specific reason but was reluctant to ask for clarification from the Central Brainstore hub as her fatigue level was high.

It was several moons later that Opal was included in the automatic inclusion into the transferred information from the discs of millennia past. She suspected the omission was due to the Central Brainstore Hub knowing of her emotional weakness, and her present inclusion was to judge if she was suitable to be readmitted. She felt detached initially which was reassuring and she fully entered into the receiving and transmitting processes.

She was connected to information which she found confusing. This was an emotion that was not acceptable but she continued to receive visual images and was able to delete any detection of unacceptable emotion by triggering her barrier.

She received more information about the Earth planet of four millennia past. There were moving pictured of underwater expanses.

There were gigantic creatures, named as dolphins, in the water moving in a mesmerising way. There was a man using words to inform the populations that they were destroying the planet. He showed the enormous sea creature with something he named as plastic caught around its body and killing it. The populations of time past had caused so much pollution in the sea that the creatures living in it were becoming threatened.

Again, Opal found herself caught up with emotions, one of which was sadness. This was a feeling that she found impossible to experience and she volunteered an immediate exit, again stating fatigue. The following session Opal undertook was one that would remain constantly with her.

The images were beautiful and so vibrant that Opal felt a peacefulness enclose her. The planet earth was full of colour and creatures in time past. Opal questioned what had caused their extinction. She absorbed the immense scenes of birds and animals moving in what looked like a natural habitat. She did not recognise any of them but wondered at the variety and differences between them. They appeared to be in constant movement, looking for food or water. Opal suspected their future was also threatened.

Suddenly another disc superseded the present one projected onto her Brainstore. She saw images of individuals within a screen. There was much violence. Opal knew she was receiving this information at the same time as it was transmitted to the other Summiters. She became detached as she could not retain the excessive images of killings, fightings and overpowering movements of aggression without activating her emotion protection to its maximum potential. She could not risk any suspicions of becoming emotionally labile.

As the number of violent images increased she realised she was becoming dulled to it. She was not familiar with being unable to understand the information transmitted to her from the Central Brainstore Hub. However, she knew, somewhere in the deepest part of her Brainstore, these were very negative images from the past millennia and further investigation was necessary to eliminate uncertainty. She was most uncomfortable with the levels of noise, colour and rapid intense movement, especially receiving realistic images of sharp weapons named as 'knives' being thrust into people. Summiter Opal had no experience to enable her to understand this assault on her Brainstore.

She hoped that, whatever the content of the next programme, it would not cause her such a depth of grief.

Nineteen

When Summiter Stone automatically transmitted another activity he experienced images consisting of individuals moving very fast. There were many of them running round something named 1500 metres. Once again there were numbers of populations watching this and making movements, waving things in the air and opening their mouths.

The image moved to a green surface on which there were about thirty people running after a globe with pointed ends. This was explained as 'rugby' and popular with the Ancients. Again there was much involvement of populations watching. There was a person supervising this activity and stopping the movements for some reason which appeared to be an infringement of the rules. Summiter 'Stones's information was instantly relayed to the Central Brainstore Hub as before and distributed to all the other Summiters.

The next activity seemed even more pointless to Summiter Opal and she watched in horror as two large men hit each other. Many of the populations watched and shouted. The fighters were wearing strange clothing and were in a cage. Opal saw blood running down their faces. The people watching had open mouths and appeared to be involved. Opal found herself wondering why the populations of so many centuries past should need to be so stimulated by this activity.

Once again,she knew her emotion barrier needed activating as she was aware her feelings of unease would be transmitted to the other Summiters. However, she felt confident that her emotion shield would protect her. As her experiences within the container grew in number she found she was feeling a growing sense of frustration at the inability of the Ancients to solve their basic problems.There was an interval before Summiter Opal was involved again. She had continued to receive all the information from the other Summiters automatically, but when they met there was no communication between them. They had received the identical materials and had all witnessed the contents of the discs. Opal thought there might have been just a small sign from one of them of a reaction. The other Summiters were behaving as decreed; detached, passive and unaffected.

It was at that moment that Summiter Opal knew there was a specific part of her own Brainstore that differed from any of the other Summiters. She knew then, with certainty, she was the only one with the capacity to activate an emotion barrier.

After seven moons had passed Summiter Opal was instructed to attend another session for research purposes.

This time she chose one from the bottom of the countless pile. The images made an impact as the content was, she was told, of a birth of a Starter 4000 years past. There was a room with a woman on a bed with a mask over her mouth. She was breathing deeply and making strange noises. Her legs were apart and, after much moaning, a head appeared between them. Someone named as a 'Nurse' pulled the Starter out and it began to breathe. Summiter Opal couldn't understand why this was the method used to replace populations.

She noticed there were people, once again, 'crying', but not with the same expressions on their faces. They were something named as 'happy' to have produced another addition to the population.

Opal asked for more information about the meaning of 'happy' and 'crying' and she was informed these were called 'feelings' or 'emotions' and not appropriate for the time present populations.

She did not feel as if she had finished the experience but decided to terminate her session anyway as she needed to think further about all the information she had received.

Many moons passed and Summiter Opal received all the container disc content from the others in the team with an increasing reluctance. She knew with certainty, she was being driven by some unknown force, to become involved with it in an individual way. She started to resent any interference from the Central Brainstore Hub. With this energy she tested her emotion barrier and found she could increase the power by intense thought processes.

When her next session was instigated she triggered her strongest emotion barrier force.

Experiencing the visual impact of the birth of a 'Starter' from four millennia past stimulated Opal into comparing the system of the present time when the embryo is developed for twenty weeks in a nutritious liquid supplied by an artificial cord. There are many robots with specific roles. The chosen 'mother' who had donated the egg and the sperm from a bank of super providers, has nothing to do apart from collect the baby after 'birth.' Robots care for all the 'Starter's needs and the mother returns to employment immediately. As there are many occupations needing consistent workers, this avoids any unacceptable situations.

Each being is constantly judged and assessed. As there are no variations allowed, promotion to a 'leadership' role is done on an age basis, all peoples being considered equally relevant. The women are almost identical to the men. We have information that many of the time present personal genetic traits were under scrutiny in millennia past and evolutionary changes already subtly altering. We have the knowledge that confusion was developing between sexual identities. The overwhelming opinion of women was to eliminate preferential decisions being made in favour of the male and therefore the logical conclusion was made to merge individuals into one sexual organism combining all the skills and functions of each. This has not been completely achieved and we still categorize men and women as having some individuality. Within several centuries we are certain that this will be the desired outcome and all peoples will be in a role consistent with the expectations of the Central Brainstore Control.

The next occasion for investigation into the contents of the massive containers undertaken by Summiter Opal was after a considerable time. She made certain that she showed no impatience. This time a specific disc was allocated. It contained details of the first time the moonplanet was visited. Of course this was of no interest apart from an historical record.

She learnt the first moonplanet visit was in 1969. The visitors wore strange white clothes and helmets and appeared to have wires and tubes attached to the moonship. It is clear that we have used our superior research techniques over many centuries to perfect our use of the resources surrounding the worldmass.

In time present all citizens must be transported to another planet at least once every six months. Once there they have to complete various tasks concerned with building living facilities for the chosen, predetermined and monitored expanding population.

Three planets have been colonised.

Twenty

To journey to another planet takes a matter of minutes as time is irrelevant. On arrival this is reversed and time is extended to the normal twenty hours of artificial daylight and twenty hours of darkness.

Travelling on earth planet is also swift and automated. A request can be made to the Central Brainstore Control. All energy is then accessed from solar storage sources if the visit is permitted.

It has been noted the research into energy was much too slow in millennia past as priority appears to have been given to other less vital outcomes. We have been addressing the storage of energy and have reached optimum levels. The Brainstore Control Hub uses its infinite prediction ability and all energy needs are met instantly.

Summiters Stone and Opal were transported to Marsplanet for six months to achieve their predetermined tasks. There were many positive outcomes expected and Stone and Opal were successful in their designated projects of water storage, meteorite re-routing, energy concentration, land reclamation and living pod design. They were returned after this mission re-energised by the successes especially as the population was stable and functioning positively. Summiter Opal had merged three Marsplanet minerals to achieve a source of nutrients necessary to maintain over eighty percent of all that was necessary for healthy life forces and growth.

It was Summiter Opal's duty again to research into the contents of the container discs. She was immediately apprehensive but, strangely, the Central Brainstore Control made no decision to terminating her involvement, probably because she had anticipated being given another session and had immediately activated her emotion barrier control at its highest level. She picked up another disc from the bottom corner of the enormous pile.

Immediately images appeared that were inexplicable to her. It was made clear that these images were of areas where food was grown in the year 2500 time past. There were vast expanses of bare, dark brown land. There were massive buildings in which animals named as cows were kept. All the movement that Summiter Opal noticed was completed by very unsophisticated robots. She found herself looking for an indication of an individual from the population but saw none. It was explained to her that all food production was automated. Populations were only involved in organising the robotic delivery systems. She wondered where all the peoples had gone.

Summiter Opal knows that in time present food production is undertaken in enormous underground units with powerful natural solar energy supplying all essential needs. No hormones are allowed and only naturally produced additives, minerals and vitamins, herbs and spices utilised. Each unit of people is allocated the necessary amount of foodstuff for a healthy lifestyle. They all earn points that can be used to obtain 'luxuries' for their living pods. As all the vital components for a balanced life are delivered to the individual living pods, there are few needs for anything extra and the definition of 'luxuries' has become redundant.

As all earth was destroyed by overuse millennia past it became unsuitable for plant growth. A few isolated parts of Africa were allowed to continue to grow food. There appeared to be a sustainable method of supporting the very small population organically but the permanent damage to the vast majority of the earth soils meant this was only temporary. We are studying this for research purposes only.

As Summiter Opal received all this complex and confusing information she, again, found herself becoming emotionally affected. She continued to experience life as it was 4000 years past.

One particular image was thrust on her Brainstore receiver and, again, it was something inexplicable even with intense concentration.

There was a small container carrying many adult and Starter populations crammed together.

These were people trying to travel to another area as they were not likely to survive if they remained in their original location. Opal watched the images as many of those in what was named 'boats' fell off or the boat sank under the rough waters. Opal received these images in disbelief. All the details were related to her in factual terms and left her with distinctly uneasy feelings which she was unable to name. There were many thousands of these peoples trying to get to safety. Many thousands did not survive.

Some time passed before she, again, was personally involved with transmitting further details from The Central Brainstore Hub. She was required to take an enforced interval for an intensive repeat of the resetting of her receptors. Although this was successful and Summiter Opal was considered to be in an acceptable condition, she suspected that the strength of her emotion barrier needed attention.

She knew, in the depths of her being, that she needed to experience all the reactions possible to the contents of the containers. She was hoping that her power over her emotional reaction levels could be activated to a higher level. As she was fulfilling her food distribution task, she received a direction to attend the container area once again.

This duty was performed and she chose a disc from a position close to one she had chosen previously. She activated her emotional barrier, anticipating she would experience another unacceptable reaction but the content she was receiving was of such impact that it was a great length of time before her Brainstore allowed her to return to normal functioning. She felt as if in a mist, floating uncontrollably with no will or choice of her movements.

The images she received were attended by a man named as Sir David Attenborough of millennia past. She became totally absorbed by the words used by this man. He was warning of disasters in future time. As she listened to the complex explanations of the self-destruction routes the populations were following, she was aware of feelings of deep sorrow entering her Brainstore.

These were, of course, filtered out by her emotional barrier control so no suspicion would fall on her. She listened and absorbed the calm and considered words that this elderly man used.

This was the man who had worked all his long life to learn about and conserve all the natural habitats of wildlife. He had studied many visual images of the Worldmass environment; peoples and living organisms both on land and at sea. He predicted impending disasters if all the world's leaders ignored the warning signs. He spoke with passion and conviction. This was the year of 2019. a time of which Opal had a growing understanding. She found herself becoming angry at the stupidity of the peoples of millennia past. Anger was a novel emotion and one which she was gradually recognising.

Feeling exhausted, she triggered her autopickup switch and returned to her pod. She knew this wouldn't cause suspicion as she had performed with perfection when visiting other planets and her reputation was at the highest level.

Twenty One

Some time passed before Opal felt she could undergo the intensity of the content of another disc.

However, as time passed, she felt an eagerness growing and promptly accepted the instruction from Central Brainstore Hub.

She approached the container eagerly and initiated another series of discs which, again, contained scenes full of profound colour and movement. She received something named as 'Music' and found herself almost unable to continue to receive the images because the intensity was so overwhelming. She knew her acceptance of all the information the Central Brainstore Hub transmitted was at a high level and found herself swaying uncontrollably to the rhythm of the auditory stimulus and was overcome by feelings of tranquillity. She had never heard sounds such as these. After some time she curtailed her receptors, and triggered her fatigue autoswitch.

She felt as if she was being owned by a multitude of new experiences in which she was eager and willing to participate but was almost overtaken by another unknown emotion.

She found another disc, hoping she would react with the same intensity, although the impact was extremely exhausting for her. This disc was, again, from the time past

2000. The images were of scenes of white ice mountains, named as ice floes. These were melting and causing many serious problems throughout the Worldmasses, with floods, hurricanes, the rising of sea levels and extreme weather temperatures becoming more regular occurrences.

The David Attenborough man was, once again, giving much information with more intense warnings of the environmental damage being thrust on all aspects of life. Suddenly, the images were shattered as the music bounced into loud, aggressive sounds. Opal was stunned by this unexpected intervention. The visual images moved to large mammals named as 'whales', swimming in enormous quantities of water. Opal was informed this was named as an 'Ocean'. There was a small whale being dragged alongside the parent whale. There were many pieces of something named as 'plastic' floating around the whales. The word 'plastic' is a word we are familiar with and we have the knowledge that it was a very damaging to the environment. There was a length of it surrounding the whale's neck. It was no longer living and the voice told us that the 'plastic' was destroying the living creatures in the seas and polluting the water. Opal recognised the calm but insistent voice of David Attenborough as he spoke with firmness and kindness but great authority.

Opal knew this information came from the Brainstore Control Hub. She continued receiving the images and associated words that she was finding increasingly impossible to retain passive as was mandatory. She watched, as evidence of millennia past, showed almost immeasurable pollution of all areas of living conditions. Opal had a growing awareness that this could have been one of the causes of the extinction of the majority of the peoples.

Summiter Opal was mesmerised by these images. She knew she must show even more care with her emotional barrier control.

She had a growing awareness that she was in a privileged position to be able to appreciate and react to all the varied and unique scenes but she knew her level of emotional involvement was increasing dramatically.

There was a space in time as the Summiters had other duties to complete.

Summiter Opal had a sudden and unusual instinct of anticipating some action unconnected to her usual routine. It felt as if a void had appeared in her Brainstore and she became uneasy as she found herself experiencing an almost obsessive need to find out more about the times of so long past. She knew the other Summiters would have her personal thoughts transferred to them individually but any of her emotional reactions would have been deleted. As time passed she was increasingly convinced that her control was total.

Consistently, she was aware of being possessed by some unidentifiable, intransigent energy which drove her, over which she had no control. At regular intervals she received all the automatic facts from the other Summiters. As present time passed into time past, she knew with absolute certainty that she was the only one possessing the ability to react emotionally.

Eventually, it was her personal duty to receive the contents of another disc.

This disc was in time past three and a half thousand years. Opal was frozen by the images she received and, again, increasingly unable to remain detached. The image was of a massive expanse of what was named as desert, consisting of minute grains named as sand. There were numerous individuals lying on the sand clothed in dull and ragged sheets. Their eyes were protruding and their limbs were like sticks. The fact given was that these populations had no food and were dying. Opal received these details without immediately feeling any reactions in her Brainstore. This was followed by an image of a thin woman with a tiny Starter in her arms. The Starter looked feeble and Opal knew it was dying. It was this image that triggered her highly charged emotional reaction and she immediately knew the barrier she was able to activate had been engaged.

Watching these images was increasingly painful to Opal as she received the information that many thousands of the populations had died because they were ignored and their needs not addressed.

Another thoughtful period followed as Opal distanced herself from the containers, fulfilling many of the other tasks, giving them her complete attention.

She was, once again, instructed to enter into researching the contents of the containers. She found she was experiencing a certain apprehension but, of course, reacted immediately to Central Control Hub's direction to avoid sanction. Inserting a disc, Opal had already anticipated becoming emotionally affected and had already activated her barrier system.

She was shown images of the young Ancients spending the majority of their time in a small area, isolated from any other humans. Opal began to understand the word 'obsession'.In an extremely distressing way, they appeared to have very little contact with others. They were looking at screens of varying sizes, for many hours at a time with blank faces. Opal, with her newly acquired ability to sense emotions, knew these were not experiencing contentment. As she continued watching she increasingly understood the importance of having human communication. It became obvious that these young peoples' interests were owned by screens of varying sizes. She felt a growing uneasiness.

Opal knew that The Central Brainstore Hub had deactivated and destroyed all knowledge of these screens. All citizens, from an early age, and are engaged in activities appropriate for their development.

In past millennia many of the population suffered from an inability of the brain to function at an acceptable level. Opal learnt from the Central Brainstore Hub that many of the Ancient Advancer stage individuals were caught up in negative activities. Opal found this impossible to understand. She knew the past leaders were in a very powerful position and questioned how the situation was ignored. From the information from Central Brainstore Hub, she was told that many of the peoples suffered from 'mental health' problems resulting in passive behaviour or antisocial and unacceptable actions. It was not possible for work to be undertaken as the individual had to spend time learning a different way of behaviour. Drugs were used to aid this recovery. Opal learnt that a term named as 'therapy' could be undertaken. Again, Opal was questioning why there seemed to be no interest in the reasons for this plague of 'mental health' problems. She then asked herself, silently, the name of which emotion she was personally experiencing.

Have you forgotten yet?
for the world's events have rumbled on since those gagged days.
Like traffic checked while at the crossing of city-ways
the haunted gap in you mind has filled with
thoughts that flow
Like clouds in the lit heaven of life,
and you're a man reprieved to go
Taking your peaceful share of Time, with joy to spare
But the past is just the same- and War's a bloody game....
Have you forgotten yet?
Look down and swear by the slain of the
War that you'll never forget.

The beginning of *'Aftermath'*
– Siegfried Sassoon

Summiter Stone transmitted the content of another disc. Summiter Opal received the content and noted that he was detached in his behaviour as he returned to is duties. It occurred to her that Summiter Stone might have the same emotion barrier ability as herself.

There seems to be an emphasis on records of disharmony. Once again the years from 2000 give us their information of living situations. We already have the knowledge that there was much aggression and fighting, caused by poverty, corruption and hatred of the religion of other societies. There were images of weapons of mass destruction at a time when many of the populations were in need. When Opal received these facts she was not surprised that there was so much unhappiness in the World's landmasses. There were many young people taking their own lives in what was then known as the developed world. We have no reaction to the word, 'developed'. We are indifferent to the terminology as it is meaningless in the context of six millennia. Summiter Opal again wondered if Summiter Stone had any opinions or thoughts about what he had just seen.

Summiter Opal was committed to her involvement with Starter nurturing. This involved being in contact with the newly-formed, ensuring all their needs were met, physically and nutritionally. She fulfilled her role as a water enabler. Each time she entered the pools with a Starter she remembered to trigger her emotion barrier. In this way she could experience true enjoyment of the feelings of weightlessness and peace. She, for the first time, knew happiness, although unable to name it.

After her allocation with the Starters was terminated she was given further duties of research into the contents of the containers.

Once again, she stimulated her maximum emotional barrier control. This gave her a satisfaction as it was the only action, she increasingly realised, that wasn't controlled by the Central Brainstore Hub.

She opened and inserted the disc. What followed was of immense importance to her as it was the initiation of an experience that would change her functioning permanently.

She saw images of people in soft clothing; she heard quiet melodic music as the two merged into coordinated movements. All the terminology was explained. She immediately understood and was absorbed by the beauty of what was named 'Ballet'. Opal was impressed by the fluidity and grace. Again, she found herself swaying to the rhythm of the music and was totally immersed in the increasing emotional effect it created. She found this disc almost impossible to terminate but knew she must follow the prescribed expectations or her involvement might cease altogether.

Afterwards, on returning to her living pod, she once again experienced a lightness of body that was helpful in lessening the negative effects of the previous disc.

Almost eagerly Summiter Opal waited for her next duty at the containers. She found herself waiting with an overwhelming eagerness as she knew something of importance was imminent.

When she was eventually instructed to research another disc she fulfilled expectations, appearing unaffected by the content. She had learnt to follow a pattern of behaviour and triggered her emotion barrier before opening the disc. She knew her reaction levels were, once again, growing in anticipation.

The disc was in the same area as the previous one and Opal knew that it was going to contain unknown and irresistible material. She activated the disc and was prepared, with no preconceptions, but only that it would be an immense experience.

What followed were scenes of many peoples carrying

what she was told were 'instruments'. There were differing sizes and shapes. What followed was unexpected. These peoples sat down in rows holding their instruments. Then a man walked to a platform and stood facing the others. He had a little stick in his hand, named as a 'baton'.

There were many other people in the large building sitting down and waiting for something to happen. They were all facing the named 'orchestra'. Then there was silence. There were a few noises from individual members but Opal received the knowledge that they were 'tuning'. Suddenly the man with the stick lifted it up and an incredible noise resulted. Opal had no words to describe it. She hoped he wasn't going to hit anyone with what was named as the 'baton'. Further information was received that the man with the baton was using it to keep all the instrument players in unison. He was named as a 'conductor'. Opal was impressed by the energy he used to wave the baton. She noticed his expression was one of total commitment and absorption.

The information given was that the orchestra was playing 'Beethoven's Third Symphony'.

What followed was an emotional attack on Opal's Brainstore and she was apprehensive that she would be terminated from the activity. She added more energy to her emotion barrier and was relieved when no intervention occurred. She was totally captivated with this experience. She felt as if she had been overtaken and immersed within an unknown space of infinity. She listened to 'Beethoven's Third Symphony' until it was finished. She couldn't move for some time as her emotional reactions had been so intense that she thought the chance of Central Control Hub being unaware of it was most unlikely. Again, she wondered whether the other Summiters had similar reactions to her own but was increasingly convinced of their total passivity.

She felt a pity for them. She knew this was an emotion but had no name for it.

Following the orchestral work, a young woman walked gracefully towards the machine. Opal thought she couldn't have been very old, perhaps an Ancient Advancer. The girl sat down at a machine which, Opal was informed, was named as a 'grand piano'. It was a large instrument with black and white rectangular, white 'keys' in lines next to each other. Overlapping them were ebony 'keys'. Quickly trying to count them, she estimated there were over eighty. Opal noticed two pedals underneath the piano within reach of the girl's feet.

There were many people watching, sitting in many rows of seats. They wore clothes that Opal was not familiar with, in many different colours. Opal was used to wearing the same garment every day and wondered what it would be like to have a choice.

After a pause, the conductor lifted his baton and the girl's hands ran over the keys rapidly. The sounds that came from them were unlike anything Opal had heard before. Simultaneously, the orchestra accompanied the piano player, coordinating the instruments perfectly. Opal found herself enclosed and owned by the 'music'. She was fascinated by the speed at which the girl moved her fingers. Eventually, the girl stopped running her fingers over the keys. Opal noted that she had five fingers on each hand. She was informed that the music was a 'Mozart Piano Concerto'. She wanted to know so much more; in fact she was desperate to know everything about the music and the person named as the composer. She felt as if there was a void in her Brainstore waiting for all lost knowledge to fill.

Eventually she managed to return to her hub, the music still playing in her sound receptors.

As she was transferring to her living pod, she felt a

detachment from her physical movements and, almost immediately, found herself entering the swimming complex. She immersed herself in the warm water and felt it brush gently against her skin. As she floated, she was smoothly pulled along in the current which was automatically adjusted to her individual needs. As the force of the water increased, her level of relaxation was also adjusted. She felt her body reacting to the involuntary muscle stimulation. Opal's response on this day was unique; one that she had never previously experienced. It was as if she was owned by a force over which she wanted no control.

Feeling calm she allowed herself to be swept along in the current. She knew there were external powers entering the water from the Central Brainstore Hub and feelings of complete detachment permeated her skin. She was convinced that if she allowed the power of the water to fulfil whatever had been programmed, the result would be benign. As the gushing water suddenly increased and waves of immense height appeared, she again stimulated her emotion barrier as it was at this immediate moment she knew she was being tested. If she showed signs of emotion at this precise time she would be destroyed. The height of the waves became bigger; so immense that, looking up, she couldn't see their summits. Again, she knew she must appear detached with the result that the Central Brainstore Control would not intervene.

She was tossed and shunted around the tops of the waves roughly. She felt like a leaf falling from one of the trees she had seen. She felt no pain but had many of the familiar emotional reactions she had recently experienced. Fear, resentment and sadness filled her, all emotions she was unable to name. There was no reaction from the Brainstore Hub. A flashing thought came to her that she was indeed capable of overpowering any negative reactions to even her most profound emotional responses.

The water suddenly calmed. A mirror-like surface surrounded her and she floated silently to the edge of the water in total tranquillity. She knew she had passed the most severe test and was able to experience any emotion without repercussions. Her only regret was her inability to identify them.

Her timecontroller indicated that she needed sustenance. She travelled to collect her adjusted quota. To all appearances she was behaving in the accepted manner.

Opal knew there were many more experiences to learn about from the contents of the containers and she was impatient to be allocated another session. She found this impatience a strange emotion, although she wasn't convinced she knew exactly what it was.She was positive the feeling was one of some agitation and was relieved when she was directed to attend another session with the containers. She did wonder if she would be tested again but had remembered to stimulate her emotion barrier to the maximum capacity as soon as her waking routine commenced.

She chose a disc from the bottom of a pile, hoping it would contain some further information which would give her unknown emotional experiences. The title on the chosen disc was 'Royal Weddings'.She was prepared for something unusual as both words were unfamiliar.

She was immediately absorbed by the content. There were so many new images with intense auditory and visual impacts, and numerous people with animated faces which she found challenging to process. There was a person in a white uniform, which Opal learnt was named a 'Wedding Dress'. There were many Ancient Learners,all in clothes that were very complicated. Opal thought the small people looked uncomfortable. There were the beautiful animals that Opal knew were named as horses, pulling a golden coach, from which the person stepped wearing the white clothes. She was helped out by a person in a red and gold uniform.

There followed the section that Opal found most wonderful. There was a Cathedral that Opal knew was where the religious people met.

The huge doors were open and the person named as a 'bride' entered holding on to the arm of another person. There was a sudden tremendous boom of what Opal knew was music. She was transfixed as the bride went down the path in the middle of many benches full of peoples all in colourful clothes and things on their heads which were strange shapes, sizes and colours.

There followed more wonderful music in between some peoples saying words that Opal didn't recognise. The music was performed by many peoples holding different instruments, similar to the concert she had witnessed.

Opal knew she was affected emotionally, in a happy interested way. Whatever the emotions were that whistled around her head she accepted with gratitude. She knew she was feeling strange towards the other Summiters and knew they had missed something of great importance.

One outcome for her was she felt reassured by the faces of the numerous peoples. For once many seemed not to need screens or to be hurting each other. Her time suddenly terminated. She was relieved as she knew the level of her emotional involvement was exceptionally high and she did not want to cause anything to prevent her barrier working. She felt her skin tingle and her Brainstore make a humming sound as if it was warning her she had overloaded her sensory receptors.

Within a short time she felt unusually carefree and full of joy. The sights and sounds she had witnessed had left her with a contentment she had never previously experienced. She returned to her living pod and accepted the sustenance that had been delivered, into her food orifice.

Later, for an unidentifiable reason, she found a feeling of dissatisfaction developing. She fulfilled the required acceptance of duties during the following twenty hours with an increasing apathy. She had never felt this emotion before and triggered her energy implant button. This took far longer than usual to respond but eventually she began to feel energised.

Opal had a growing feeling she was missing something in her day- to -day existence. She imagined actually touching one of the other Summiters gently with her hands and if there would be a reaction of any kind. She suspected the response would be detachment. She also found words entering her head and her tiny mouth trying to articulate them. She listened intently to these words. Her narrow throat felt as if it was being scratched. She was unable to translate the words but was impressed that, once more, she was experiencing something that no other Summiter ever had. She felt special and unique. What if one of the other Summiters touched her, softly; held her hand or looked at her in an emotional way, with the contact she had seen pass between the Ancients? She knew with certainty what her own reaction would be.

Twenty Two

Some time passed and Opal received all the images from the other Summiters. Strangely, there were none that had the same intense effect on her as when she was personally involved. She continued to follow her predetermined routine but was aware of the previously experienced apathy coursing around her body. This was immediately nullified when she received instructions to attend another session with the containers.

The choice of the disc had been decided. The image was of a person with what was named as a 'pen' putting marks on a piece of white material. This activity was named 'writing'. Opal watched enviously, wishing she could take part. Only having three fingers would be a handicap but 'writing' was a skill she would love to try. It wouldn't matter if she failed as it was the actual technique that appealed to her. She knew the groups of black shapes were named as 'words'. She learnt that these were formed into sentences and were the process by which information was given and connections instigated between peoples. She thought this was a truly wonderful skill owned by the Ancients.

Another disc was entered into her Brainstore, this time without her being given a choice. She accepted this eagerly, only privately questioning why no freedom to choose a disc herself was granted.

What followed was another profound experience.

There was a building named 'theatre' and there was, on a platform, peoples named as 'actors'. Opal listened to thousands of words being spoken by these actors. She was informed they were pretending to be other characters in order to act out a situation. The function of this was to entertain the peoples watching, of whom there were many, sitting on seats facing the platform, or 'stage' as Opal was to learn. Many unusual clothes were worn. Opal listened to the words and became fascinated by the way the individuals responded to each other. There was an intriguing 'script' with words sounding much like the music she had experienced, full of rhythms and unfamiliar patterns. Opal responded to the performance with a level of inquisitiveness that she had become used to and followed the long sequences avidly. There was a man wanting to be a leader named as a 'king'. There were many angry situations but, after much time, it appeared to end in a satisfactory manner. The peoples all hit their five-fingered hands together loudly. Opal realised this meant they had enjoyed the performance. An image of what looked like a large thin book appeared on Opal's receptor. There was a long list of all the actors that had appeared in the performance. The words were written by a man named as Shakespeare. Opal would have liked to have found out more about the language she had heard. It was of an unusual but compelling sequence of sounds and patterns to her ears and she wanted to learn more. Her session was terminated. Opal knew she had activated her emotion barrier but was too full of the newly acquired information to think anything was wrong.

She suddenly noted that she had activated her emotion barrier to a minimal level only. She knew her eagerness to become involved in the contents of the discs had made her careless. Her channels with all the other Summiters remained fully functioning but there were still no reactions from them.

There were several tasks needing Opal's attention. Her duties with the Starters filled her time. She had many targets to reach and her concentration on these helped to ease the impatience which she found unpleasant. She continuously monitored her emotion barrier. Eventually she was directed to attend the containers once again. She activated her emotion barrier to the strongest level, feeling apprehensive that she might be losing this essential facility.

Opal selected the disc that appeared to be sliding towards her. She entered it into her Brainstore and was immediately confused by some of the content. Further information was given about the sequence of script.

She received the interpretation of the letters C.N.D. which appeared on a white flag in black lettering. She wanted to know what this signified.

'Campaign for Nuclear Disarmament' had no meaning at this point and she waited for further explanation. Further details were given and she saw images of many peoples in the years 1950 onwards protesting against nuclear weapons. Opal wanted more information and was given an increasing understanding of nuclear power. This, once used for providing energy, left a lethal and hazardous residue, which caused anxiety, as the storage of it could prove unreliable. The 'Nuclear Waste' endured for thousands of years. Opal found herself consistently questioning the actions of these Ancients. The emotion of frustration was uppermost and she wished she could revert to the previous discs of music, performance and elation. This was not to happen and she returned to her living pod feeling as if her emotions had been sedated.

However, to ease the tautness in her, Opal was eager to submerge herself in water and accessed it immediately.

Lying on her back she closed her sight receptors and allowed the water to stroke her outer skin as she floated freely.

She started moving her limbs, imagining the music of Mozart. Very rapidly feelings of calm overtook her. She allowed herself added time as a reluctance to return to her pod invaded her thoughts. The Central Control Hub gave instant instruction and she found herself moved in time immediate to her living hub. She was left with a strong sense of losing part of herself.

Almost immediately, she was instructed by the Central Brainstore Hub to attend her completion of physical attainment assessment. Most of this was automatic and fulfilled by programmed robotic sensors. At random times a total appraisal was carried out to ensure the individual Summiter was responding perfectly to all expectations. Opal instigated her most powerful emotion barrier as this was the only area in which she could fail. She knew she appeared in total control and was confident when she received the expected signal to return to her duties.

Very quickly she was expected to research another container disc. She instigated this immediately and was allowed to choose a disc from the furthest corner of the immense container. She hoped for another experience similar to those of the previous occasion.

The contents of the disc were extremely stimulating. There were many peoples wearing brilliantly coloured clothes. Some were dancing, some carried banners on which there were words foreign to her until the information was transmitted to her Brainstore. There was music and dancing and an atmosphere of happiness. Opal recognised this feeling as an emotion and decided not to bother with trying to name it, but just let it invade her body.

The peoples were celebrating something named as 'Gay Pride'. Millennia time past there were many peoples with confusing sexual identities. By drawing attention to this, the other peoples became more tolerant. Summiter Opal knew that in time present there were no situations comparable to this. All of the present peoples have a function which does not depend on any sexual orientation.

Opal knew the Summiters were almost identical because the sexes were almost merged. She had, however, noted two or more people communicating and touching one another, with happy expressions. She thought this was preferable to not knowing a gender and being free to respond to others in any way.

As she entered the disc into her Brainstore she had turned to face the side of the container. There was Summiter Bone, looking intently at her. She nodded but Summiter Bone continued to watch her, motionless. Opal felt an emptiness surround her and kept very still. She knew Summiter Bone was receiving identical images and she deliberately continued to appear in an acceptable and static mode, absorbing all the content and trying to ignore the presence of the other Summiter.

The music was, once again, lively and stimulating. Opal found her flat feet were bouncing on the ground in time with the beat. She assessed and increased the power of her emotion barrier and knew she must enjoy the sensation of happiness. Many of the peoples dancing and walking in the procession played instruments. The faces were full of life, showing high levels of energy. If Summiter Bone was unable to appreciate the music, Opal thought, that was unfortunate but she was unable to prevent herself from entering into the experience. She was extremely aware of his presence and sensed he was watching her with an unknown purpose. She found herself overtaken by the different types of music she was receiving and ignored any slight warning that Summiter Bone emitted.

She remained as long as she thought advisable but knew she was becoming careless as she noticed Summiter Bone suddenly disappearing. She felt detached about his absence. She knew she'd felt as if she could lose control and dance herself but her flat feet were heavy and stiff. She wondered what reaction Summiter Bone had felt but suspected he was unable to feel anything at all. She reminded herself that water could give her a similar emotional fulfilment and transported herself to the facility once again. Only one Summiter was permitted at each session. Opal thought it might have been interesting to have somebody else with her, but gave herself up to the familiar peaceful experience. Weightlessness overtook any questions she might have needed answering and all tightness of her body dissipated into the water. Opal thought it might be a good time to activate her self-destruct switch. Her relaxation levels were so complete, both body and mind; a mind until recently that had been content to accept everything that was demanded from her. As she lay in the water she considered all the many different images to which she had been exposed. She asked herself if she really was the only being with the ability to 'feel' and, if so, what was the logic behind it.

Was she being secretly assessed or identified as a threat to the populations? Was the fact that she had an emotion barrier now in the Central Control Hub's possession? Opal knew the amount of information they had at their command was total.

The following session she was instructed to attend came immediately after Opal had completed the water routine. She was eager to learn anything at all about the sequential history of the past.

She received an increasing amount of information about the Ancients' behaviours and had pity for them. Not because of any confusion about which gender they possessed but the waste of the enormous amount of energy they had to devote to feeling accepted. She curtailed the session herself. There was nothing she could learn from this disc, apart from the growth of tolerance that the Ancients appeared to be developing.

Many duties awaited Summiter Opal and she fulfilled her responsibilities with a growing eagerness. She knew she was beginning to enjoy the privileges of the time present as well as learning about the Ancients. There were so many unknown emotions to welcome and her energy to encounter them was boundless.

She knew with ever-increasing certainty that she was the only Summiter to have the capacity of possessing emotions. She began to understand this as an ability to react to visual and physical stimulation. When in contact with the other Summiters she functioned with the accepted, emotionless and automatic procedures. Her relief was tangible, but only to herself.

She was increasingly aware that she was experiencing many more emotional responses, even in her day to day duties. She vowed to activate her barrier to the highest level on waking every day even if not on container duty. She was eager to attach a name to the unfamiliar feelings, but was confused by the quantity. Some were pleasurable and others left her with feelings of intense sadness. She could not ask the Central Control Hub to identify these emotions as suspicion would be immediately generated.

One particular reaction to the disc contents was emptiness. She named this herself and made the decision to invent names each time she found herself emotionally affected.

Twenty Three

Once again it was time for her to visit another planet and she prepared herself, with detachment, to fulfil all that was expected of her. She found herself questioning the population's ways, knowing they were all predetermined, similar to those on the Earthmass. She observed the planets' peoples and noticed how there was no communication between them and no signs of reactions. She had never been in a position before to question the conditions in which she lived.

All activities were fulfilled with no expression of what Opal had named as 'joy'. She realised The Summiters, in their personal situations, had no need for any emotional involvement at all. She questioned whether this was a condition she would willingly return to if the situation demanded it.

On returning to planet Earth, she was eager to further her research into the containers. She named this feeling 'intensity'. Eventually, she was directed to fulfil this duty and proceeded to the area where the discs had been located. Choosing one at the surface and entering it into her Brainstore, she recognised the beautiful animals from a previous disc.

The horses were on a flat, green surface eating. This was named as 'grass'. The horses appeared calm and contented and Opal noticed there were no metal bars through their mouths or on their feet. Some young Learners approached the horses which stood motionless. Opal couldn't understand what followed. The Ancient Learners had brushes in their hands and they very cautiously started to brush the coats of the horses. One Learner gently stroked one of the horses on its neck, rather nervously. Information came through to Opal's Brainstore. These Ancient Learners were not allowed with others as they were unable to function in an acceptable way. They were attending these 'stables' with the horses as it was one method by which these young Learners could adapt their behaviour. Opal learnt that the results from this treatment were positive and the Ancient Learners loved to be in the company of these magnificent creatures. Eventually they were allowed back with the other Learners. Opal wanted to ask questions but knew these would be considered abnormal. If she was indeed under suspicion any probing would only increase any doubt about her functioning.

Opal watched the faces of the young people and she was filled with yet another new emotion. She named this as 'quietness'. Although not content with this word, she was at a loss to access one that would satisfy her. She also felt a sadness for these Learners who, she was informed, were disruptive and antisocial. Watching their sensitive but slightly reluctant reactions to the horses made her think that perhaps the previous environment in which they were placed was at fault.

When she left the container, she noticed Summiter Bone again, standing impassively, apparently watching her. Her accidental acknowledgement was ignored and she returned quickly to her pod, regretting her weak attempt at communicating with another Summiter physically, something never permitted.

She was left with yet another unnamed emotion.

When she was directed to attend another session she activated her barrier, again, to the strongest level, anticipating something immense was about to be presented.

Her predictions proved accurate.

She opened and entered the disc to be instantly assaulted by a wave of the previously named 'Music'. She was informed the 'musical' was named as 'Mama Mia'. The effect the music had on her was intense. She felt as if she had been attacked by an earthquake. There was a plethora of colour, noise, music, and people dancing. The overall impression she received was again of intense 'joy'. She couldn't absorb the actions that were happening between the individuals but knew certain problems were being solved. After the disc ended she kept very still and found any movement impossible. The intensity that filled her whole being was overpowering and she didn't want it to stop.

Returning to her pod Opal thought of the Ancient peoples and the richness of experiences they had all around them. Even with the terrible parts of their existence, there must have been solutions that could have been found.

The visual histories that Opal was learning about had an intensity for which she wanted to indulge herself personally. There were so many facts that Opal needed to learn and she was determined to take every opportunity to avail herself of them. Her previous thought of ending her duties as a Summiter faded away. After her previous session she felt intensely fatigued and was forced to trigger her autopickup. She was apprehensive the Central Brainstore control might be alerted to her unusual reactions to the contents of the discs, even though she had activated her emotion barrier to the highest level.

Another allocated time was spent fulfilling responsibilities unconnected to researching the contents of the containers.

Opal controlled herself after feelings of impatience super-imposed themselves on her thoughts. This reaction was happening more frequently and she found her ability to ignore it increasing. Although she was aware that her functioning would be considered unacceptable if it became known by the Central Control Hub, her attention to the importance of initiating her emotion control barrier increased in frequency and intensity.

Opal was in complete possession of the knowledge that there were no circumstances under which she would consider returning to her previous state of what she considered a mechanical existence. She didn't even give this a second thought. Having experienced different emotions, her need for an extension of these almost became an obsession.

It seemed an age before she was directed to attend another research session in the contents of the containers. She was especially efficient when activating her personal emotion barrier. She felt controlled and impassive as she opened another disc and entered it into her Brainstore. Initially she was confused at what she received. There was an enormous room with frames of many sizes on the wall. There were many peoples standing looking at what was contained in the frames.

Opal watched closely as she received the images. It took her some time before she comprehended what exactly it was she was receiving. Eventually she realised that the peoples were looking very closely at what was in the frames. Opal became absorbed by the images, named as 'Paintings'. They were completed by eminent 'artists'. The 'artists' were mentioned many times as information was given about the paintings, the artists and their histories. There were paintings named as 'portraits' which were of peoples of long past, even prior to the Ancients. The clothing was very different, colourful and intricate from those which Opal was familiar;

the hair was something she had never seen. Opal's interest grew as she knew she was looking at the results of incredible skills. She wanted to know how these paintings were made and what was used but was reluctant to ask Central Control Hub to access this information in case it provoked suspicion. She spent the maximum time she was permitted studying the contents of the pictures, the outcome being a need to find out more.

She knew all the other Summiters throughout the Worldmass would have simultaneously received contents from the disc she had seen and was perplexed that there was not a single response from them. They continued to have total detachment. Opal knew they were missing something incredibly important. This emotion she repeatedly named as 'empty'. She thought this word described their lack of reaction to the latest disc accurately. For the following prescribed amount of time Opal was in one of the research hubs donating a gene. Gene donation was a regular undertaking and considered an honour as only those of a superior quality were stored for future use. She found herself questioning, once again, the detachment by which this was robotically achieved and found herself wishing there could have been some physical contact with other Summiters. She had noticed that the Ancients used words to communicate with each other occasionally and could be seen touching and using words between them.

She was relieved to be instructed to attend the container area once again. Picking up the nearest, that seemed to jump up at her, she had a premonition the contents would again stimulate her emotions.

There was an image of many peoples. For the first time she noticed that they were of varying coloured skins some much darker than others. Her constant familiarity with her own surrounding peoples had deadened her awareness of colour. All the peoples on Earthmass and Moonmass had brownish skins. Opal decided to look more closely at these peoples from millennia past. Their hearing mechanisms were prominent as were the sight organs. Opal had decided that the large holes in the bottom of the face were where the 'words' came from and were used to make a connection to others of the peoples. Wanting to learn more, she chose another disc hoping it would give her the information she wanted, even though she wasn't sure what it was she was looking for.

Almost immediately she received images of these different coloured peoples on a large area of green. Immediately music filled her receptors and the peoples moved in time with the rhythm. All the faces were of a calmness to which Opal responded. She checked her emotion barrier as she predicted her responses were about to be engaged at a high level.

The music continued at an increasing speed and the peoples moved faster and faster, with hands and arms waving in the air. Opal joined in, not caring if the other Summiters noted her inexplicable and clumsy actions. She was totally absorbed in the ever-changing music and rhythms and was filled with another nameless emotion. She was receptive to the images of these peoples, that could fight and show aggression, and could also show cooperation and peacefulness. Opal knew the present emotion was one she enjoyed. She wanted to be able to attach a name to the variety of feelings she had experienced but knew this would not be permitted. Eventually she returned to her pod, again with a lightness about her.

The following sunrise Opal sprung out of her sleeping pad and, as much as her flat feet would permit, danced light-footedly over to the opening in her pod.

There was an instruction for her to go immediately to the containers as there was an item there for her to investigate.

This direction gave her one of her newly acquired feelings of happiness, and she covered the distance to the containers rapidly.

Opal had forgotten to activate her control barrier.

She entered the container and picked up a disc that appeared to be waiting, entering it into her Brainstore but immediately felt disappointment.

The disc was a record of another war, between the years 2014 and 2018. There were millions killed, many too injured to be recognised and even more left with irreparable mental health. Many areas of the world were involved, routinely trained to butcher other humans.

Opal saw images of fields of blood, countless dead and dying, bodies writhing in mud and countless unrecognisable body parts. As she became increasingly horrified she was drawn into a profound depth of sadness and despair, two emotions she recognised immediately.

She knew these peoples had possessed a chance to invent, cooperate, create, listen and talk to each other and develop the amazing creative opportunities surrounding them.

She put her hand up to her cheek as she felt something wet coming out of her eyes and sliding down her face.

In an instant there was a flashing light, burning into her skin. There was no sound but an intense smell of burning flesh.

Opal knew, instantly, this was a sign that she was destroyed.

The End